"What's wrong?" Skeeter asked her mother, uncertain.

Rita swiped a tissue over her eyes, reached out and hugged her daughter. "I'm crying because I'm happy."

"But you're okay?" Skeeter pressed, confused.

Rita hugged her again and gave a brisk nod. "I'm more than okay. I'm wonderful. I'm going to open my own bakery."

Rita flashed Brooks a smile that thanked him for his caring, his friendship, his support and maybe more.

"This makes our celebration tonight doubly sweet."

"It does."

Rita sailed into his arms and hugged him, holding tight, feeling more right and natu~~ral~~ than he had hoped and dreamed fo~~r~~. "Thank you."

"For what?"

Her smile said more ~~than~~. "Everything."

His heart burst wide op~~en, wanti~~ng her, her family. Holding her, cher~~ishi~~ng her—this was the future he'd wanted and needed without knowing it.

Books by Ruth Logan Herne

Love Inspired

Winter's End
Waiting Out the Storm
Made to Order Family

RUTH LOGAN HERNE

Born into poverty, Ruth puts great stock in one of her favorite Ben Franklinisms: "Having been poor is no shame. Being ashamed of it is." With God-given appreciation for the amazing opportunities abounding in our land, Ruth finds simple gifts in the everyday blessings of smudge-faced small children, bright flowers, fresh baked goods, good friends, family, puppies and higher education. She believes a good woman should never fear dirt, snakes or spiders, all of which like to infest her aged farmhouse, necessitating a good pair of tongs for extracting the snakes, a flat-bottomed shoe for the spiders, and the dirt....

Simply put, she's learned that some things aren't worth fretting about! If you laugh in the face of dust and love to talk about God, men, romance, great shoes and wonderful food, feel free to contact Ruth through her Web site at www.ruthloganherne.com.

Made to Order Family
Ruth Logan Herne

Steeple
Hill®

Published by Steeple Hill Books™

STEEPLE HILL BOOKS

Steeple Hill®

Recycling programs for this product may not exist in your area.

ISBN-13: 978-0-373-87623-5

MADE TO ORDER FAMILY

Copyright © 2010 by Ruth M. Blodgett

www.SteepleHill.com

Printed in U.S.A.

And be not drunk with wine, wherein is excess;
but be filled with the Spirit.
—*Ephesians* 5:18

This book is dedicated to my beautiful girls,
Sarah, Mandy, Beth, Lacey and Karen. I hope my
love inspires your continued strength and faith as
motherhood offers interesting challenges and grace.
Just remember that Cousin Ann in
Understood Betsy is a GREAT role model.
Seriously.

Acknowledgments

Special thanks to the local members of Alcoholics
Anonymous whose ongoing struggles and strengths
helped me create this story, and to the communities
of Canton, Potsdam, Pierrepont and Malone for
their graciousness. Special thanks to the good
Sisters of St. Joseph, especially Sr. Mariel from
Nazareth Academy, whose belief in me never
wavered. Thanks to my dad who gave me a Wilton
cake-decorating book when I was sixteen. Thus
began a long career of creating beautiful cakes
and pastries. His love of baking became mine.
Special appreciation to Mark Bowden, author of
Black Hawk Down, and Eric Haney, author of
*Inside Delta Force: The Story of America's Elite
Counterterrorist Unit,* two wonderful depictions of
life in Special Forces.

Chapter One

Rita Slocum worked to envision every possible reason why she shouldn't quit her job right now, pack it in and call it a day.

Three good reasons came to mind. Liv, Brett and Skeeter, her beautiful children, three amazing gifts from God that had already suffered from their parents' host of bad choices.

Never again would she compromise their happiness.

Crossing the grocery-store parking lot, she inhaled a breath of brisk, clean, North Country spring air, gave herself a quick kick in the behind and brought to mind all she should be grateful for. Her kids. Her faith. Her home.

Her sobriety.

She fingered the bronze one-year chip she kept tucked in a pants pocket, a valid reminder of three hundred and sixty-five days of *good* choices, of strengthening values, each day chasing the pervasive shadows of drunkenness further into oblivion.

Stronger now, she refused to be fooled. Once sober, she'd studied her problem and couldn't excuse her share of the blame. It would be easy to slough things off on circumstance and depression, justify that first drink. Then the next and the next and so on.

But Rita recognized her primary responsibility in the whole mess. Sure, her life had tanked emotionally, morally and financially with her late husband's crimes and suicide, but she'd had other choices.

She'd made the wrong ones then. She'd make the right ones now.

Despite the soap opera prevailing in her current job, her kids came first. Their strength. Their faith. Their well-being. No more messing them up.

God grant me the serenity to accept the things I cannot change, the courage to change the things I can and the wisdom to know the difference.

Wonderful words, sweet and succinct. Perfect for an alcoholic's soul.

And even though today was bad, a definitive two on a scale of one to ten, most days weren't too awful, and she'd learned a great deal by working in a commercial bakery that supplied fresh bread, cakes, desserts and rolls to grocery-store shoppers.

It wasn't her dream job. No, that option lay dust-riddled alongside her computer, fact sheets for a bakery of her own, a sweetshop that called to passersby from a delectable window showcasing mouthwatering treats.

Someday.

Rita refused to be cowed by the unlikelihood of that development. For the moment she was working a no-glory job, following orders, obeying company policy on weight, ratio, freshness and back stock of quick-selling items.

It paid the bills and that was reason enough to stay—creditors were ever-present baggage from her former life. Still, her business degree from SUNY Albany prompted her to do more than follow someone else's orders, a quality she should have clung to during her marriage to Tom Slocum.

Oops.

Settling behind the wheel, she pondered her angst. Not bad enough to grab Kim, her AA sponsor, but she wanted to talk with someone who'd listen and not condemn, commiserate but not feed into her funk. Recovering alcoholics couldn't afford to bask in self-pity, ever.

Brooks.

The tall, broad-chested, sandy-haired woodcrafter with deep

gray eyes would listen. He always did. And then he'd set her straight, a trait she could do without some days. The reality of that inspired a smile. Brooks' honesty matched his integrity. Great qualities in a man.

Unless she was the target of said honesty, in which case he could take his calm, confident perceptions and bury them in his ever-present sawdust bucket.

Checking her watch, she steered the car toward Grasse Bend. Plenty of time to stop in before Skeeter's bus dropped her off at home in Potsdam, and she had to drive through Grasse Bend anyway.

Kind of.

She fought the invading flush, turned the air-conditioning to high despite the cool day and let the chilled air bathe her skin, her face. Brooks was a friend, a know-it-all one at that, a guy whose very being screamed "loner," and that's where they'd leave things. No risk, no worry.

Perfect.

"I want to quit. To walk away without a second glance and never look back. Your mission, Brooks Harriman, should you choose to accept it, is to talk me out of it."

Rita's announcement lifted Brooks' head. He glanced from the tiny, green-tipped paintbrush to the etched scroll accenting the antiqued credenza holding center stage in his "clean" room, the area designated for finishing applications, then back to her, appraising. "Hold that thought."

A smile tempted her mouth. She walked forward, more confident than she'd been last summer. Angled light bounced off ash-blond hair. Her cross necklace danced brightly in the slanted spring beam. He sensed her approval of his painstaking work before she walked toward the back of the room to greet his apprentice as he applied tung oil to a deacon's bench.

"Hey, Mick."

"Rita." Mick's low voice greeted her while his broad hands worked oil into the receptive oak, the grain leaping to life with his attentions. "How're you doing?"

Filling the etch with forest green, Brooks imagined her grimace. "Frustrated, peeved, disgruntled. Take your pick."

Brooks couldn't resist. "Whiny. Complaining. Petulant."

"I don't recall listing those."

He smiled. "Nevertheless."

"None of the above," she retorted. "And since you're working on something requiring a level of care, I suggest you pay mind to it."

"Ouch." His smile turned into a grin. "There's coffee in the pot."

Rita Slocum only drank tea. He knew it, but offered coffee anyway. It was an old game from her early days in AA, when he'd squire her for old-fashioned one-on-one. Bad enough to be a single mother with a drinking problem, but a single mother with a drinking problem in the North Country, well...

That was tough. There were no secrets in the small towns littering Route 11. But she'd made it so far and today's crisis wasn't serious or she'd have called Kim to talk it out, fight the temptation, view her choices and choose.

Her presence pushed Brooks to hurry. He dismissed the urge. Fluid green followed his strokes, filling the angles and curves. Short minutes later, he sat back, satisfied. "Done."

"I love it."

He'd sensed her approach, the scent of baked apples and cinnamon teasing his nose, tweaking awareness. He looked up. "How's your tea?" His eyes swept the foam cup, the telltale tag hanging outside.

"Wonderful. Soothing. Sweet."

He'd stocked up on various brands for when she required a sounding board. Her hair swung forward as she examined the piece, the fruity scent light and flirtatious, a delightful combination. Her sky-blue eyes twinkled. "I'm not even going to ask what something like that goes for," she quipped, admiring.

Brooks nodded. The German-style dresser was dear. "This wouldn't blend with your things anyway, would it?"

"At some point in time, when the term 'discretionary funds' reenters my vocabulary, my things will change," she promised.

She pressed her lips thin, musing. "For the moment, I'm content with the scuffed-up remnants of raising three kids."

Brooks envisioned Brett's soccer ball thumping against the finished sideboard. Drawers stuffed with disjointed game pieces. Skeeter using it as a support for her gymnastic maneuvers. Olivia...

At fifteen, Liv was probably the only one besides Rita who would treat the stylish cabinet with any level of respect. He bit back a sigh inspired by his thoughts and his early morning wake-up call. "In your particular case, I think refurbishing should stay on the back burner for a decade. Maybe two."

"For years those kids weren't allowed to live in their own house. Be creative," she told him. "Tom wasn't comfortable with disorder."

Brooks stiffened at the mention of Rita's late husband, a man who'd engineered a well-disguised Ponzi scheme that bilked money from innocent investors, then killed himself rather than face charges, leaving Rita more baggage than anyone should have to handle. Ever.

Rita didn't notice his reaction. As her finger traced the sweep of the beautiful sideboard, she lifted her shoulders. "With Brett and Liv both teenagers, they'll be gone before you know it. Plenty of time for change coming."

Brooks wiped his hands on a tack rag, stood and moved to the sink to wash up, weighing her words. Rita had learned to embrace change out of necessity, a brave move for a woman alone, a single mother to boot.

Whereas he'd run fast and hard, disappearing into oblivion when the going got tough. Polar opposites to the max.

He stretched his shoulders, rolling the joints to ease the stiffening that accompanied detail work. "So. What are we quitting?"

"Mindless work a trained monkey could do," Rita groused.

"Trained monkeys are scarce hereabouts." He poured coffee, eyed the density, scowled and added cream. "We could import some."

"There's little imagination or thought that goes into industrial baking," Rita expounded, leaning against a sturdy, unfinished logged bedstead. Her blue jeans, thin and baggy, were standard wear in the bakery. "Every cake is like every other, don't even think you can special order a combination that isn't in the book because you can't, and the custard filling tastes like chemical waste."

"It sells."

"Because there are no alternatives," she spouted, eyes flashing. "If the cheesecake cracks, they dummy it with extra topping and sell it anyway, at full price." Her voice rose. "And the crème horns? The filling comes in a box. You measure out x, add y and z and voilà! White crème filling."

"There's another way?" She ignored the humor in his tone. Didn't note the lift to his brow, the hint of a smile.

"The right way. The way it should be done, would be done if I were running the place." Arching a dark brow that contrasted with her light hair and eyes, she played her trump card. "To top it all off? Add insult to injury?"

He fought a grin and nodded, the gesture inviting her to continue.

"The cannoli filling comes from a can."

"No."

"Yes!"

The earnestness of her expression made him lose constraint. He grinned. "Who'd have thought?"

Uh-oh. The grin made her huffy. She set her tea on his workbench with an uncharacteristic thump. "Never mind, Brooks. I shouldn't have come."

"Why did you?"

"I..." His question caught her off guard. She fingered the collar of her knit shirt, nonplussed, her gaze searching his.

Mick hid a chuckle beneath a cough.

Brooks met her look, unflinching, rock solid. "Reet?"

The telltale blush traveled her throat, her cheeks. She turned toward the door. He stilled her with a gentle hand on her arm. "Open your own place. You've talked of it often enough."

"I can't."

"You don't know that."

"I do," she corrected him. "I've done my homework on this. I've scoped out costs versus income, possible locations, equipment requirements, licenses, refurbishing. The start-up costs are prohibitive and no lending institution worth its salt is going to front a loan to a drunk with a pile of bills, three kids and no money."

"What have you got to lose by filling out the applications, trying every angle?"

"Besides my self-respect and my sobriety?" She stared beyond his shoulder, gnawed her lip and drew her gaze back to his. "Rejection scares me. A lot."

Her admission didn't surprise Brooks. Rita's lack of self-esteem was a big part of what had pushed her into the alcoholic abyss that almost tore apart her family. Thankfully her sister-in-law Sarah had stepped in to take charge of the kids before Rita sought recovery the previous spring. Otherwise they'd have been wrenched apart and put in foster homes, another family gone bad.

But that hadn't happened. Instead the kids had spent the summer working on Sarah's sheep farm while Rita faced her demons and won.

God's hand at work. Brooks might never step foot into a church, but he recognized God's might and power in this particular situation. And despite his nonattendance, Brooks knew his beliefs to be as strong and ardent as most churchgoers, probably more than some. He served one God, one Almighty, the maker of heaven and earth. He just handled it a bit differently from everyone else on the planet.

Singular. Unfettered. Independent.

He prayed one-on-one, lived alone and ran his own business with no one to answer to.

Ordered. Structured. Organized to the max.

The loner profile worked for him, offering a shield of protection that he'd erected nearly a dozen years back. So far, so good. But not so easy when Rita came around. Something about her heightened his senses, awakening possibilities he'd buried long ago.

But he hadn't served as a Delta commander in the army for nothing. Brooks was adept at identifying and administrating, the sorting techniques intrinsic to success in battle. How weird was it that he needed those skills around Rita?

He dipped his chin and gave her arm an encouraging squeeze. "Things are different now. You're stronger. You've had over a year without a lapse of sobriety, you've taken a job that's helped strengthen your résumé when you do apply for bakery funding and I expect you've learned a thing or two about commercial baking in the process."

"A lot, actually."

"Then put that knowledge to good use. Draw up a prospectus."

"I already did," she admitted.

Brooks grinned. "Good girl. Now fill out some applications. Give it a shot. You've got a lot of people behind you, believing in you. You can do this."

Could she, Rita wondered? At that moment her answer was yes, Brooks' words bolstering her confidence.

Brooks Harriman didn't blow sunshine carelessly. Not now, not ever. He shot straight from the hip, his analysis unjaded and unbiased. That honesty won him respect in their tight-knit community, a precious commodity in the North County. In an area that courted winter seven months of the year, stoicism was held in high regard.

But tiny spring leaves dappled the afternoon sun with dancing shadow, their Kelly-green newness refreshing. Rita clutched her tea with one hand while the other fingered the one-year chip in her pocket. "You really think I can do this?"

His expression defined confidence. "I know you can do this. And I'll be glad to help with any and all refurbishing when you get approval and pick a site."

"There's a really sweet store available in Canton," Rita told him. The admission brought heat to her cheeks, as if she'd done something wrong in checking things out, having the audacity to believe in herself.

She gave herself an inward shake, burying the insecurities that challenged her faith in God and herself.

Change the things you can....

The words buoyed her in their simplicity.

Maybe she *could* do this.

Brooks leaned in, the scent of wood shavings and oil-based paint tickling her nose, playing havoc with her thoughts. "Coffee tonight, after Brett's game?"

Brett's travel team had a game in Canton tonight, and while Brooks wasn't a big fan of Skeeter's gymnastics performances and the accompanying histrionics, he enjoyed watching Brett's soccer matches.

"No."

"Tea, then?"

His teasing tone inspired a smile and a softer response. "I can't. I've got to get Brett and Skeeter home. Spring games on school nights are always a killer."

"Oh. Of course." Brooks replied as if he understood the time frame, but he didn't. Not really. Kid bedtimes were something he'd never had to deal with, thanks to his brother.

She walked to the door, sure-footed, more poised and confident than she'd been last summer. Back then a confrontation like this would have sent her into duck-and-cover mode. Not anymore.

She was doing well. She had her first-year chip, the bronze medallion inscribed with the sacred words of sobriety, The Serenity Prayer.

Brooks lived by that prayer, a solid credo. Over a decade ago he'd recognized what he couldn't change, so he grasped the courage to change what he could, his location. He'd come north to start anew, and he had.

Thoughts of Baltimore invaded the peaceful afternoon. His parents. His brother. Amy and her deception.

Brooks shoved them aside. He'd left the Inner Harbor because he had no choice, not after what they'd done. His faith, his focus and his freedom had been at stake, three concepts he held dear.

Family?

Um…not so much. Not since he realized that his fiancée was pregnant with his brother's child. While Brooks had been commanding men in the desert sands of Iraq, Amy and Paul had trysted in Maryland. Instead of being the model American family Brooks held in his heart, the Harrimans had been reduced to a Jerry Springer episode.

When Rita was around, a whisper of the man he'd been flickered to life. Captain Brooks Harriman, a soldier, a fighter, a special operative trained to make the most of a given situation.

His skills failed him in Baltimore. He'd been unable to separate the physical from the emotional, and had let the combination tumble him into the dark pit of alcoholism, until Sgt. Greg Callahan of the Baltimore Police Department dragged him up and out of the gutter, then became his AA sponsor.

Callahan's example as a sponsor and a man inspired Brooks. And he'd been dry for nearly a dozen years. At forty-two, he'd been spinning his wheels for a long time.

Too long, Brooks decided, watching Rita climb into her car, her hair bright with afternoon sun. Christ had promised life to the full, his words giving hope to gathered throngs.

When Rita was around, the sweet scent of cinnamon-soaked apples teasing his senses, that fullness seemed possible. Plausible. Add three kids to the mix…

Brooks passed a hand along the nape of his neck as Rita's car curved north. Her kids couldn't afford any more mistakes. Neither could she. But life without chances wasn't really life, and right now Brooks was ready to reach for the gold ring he'd missed twelve years before. Now if he could just convince Rita…

A slight smile tugged his lips. He'd managed to oversee covert operations, lead men into battle and engineer the behind-the-scenes cyber breakdown of Iraqi military software, disabling their computerized navigation systems. One sweet, thirty-eight year old single mother shouldn't be all that hard.

Right?

Chapter Two

"I hate those shoes." Skeeter's tone sounded like Rita's had earlier. Rita grimaced, recognizing the parallel. "They're ugly."

"Then wear your sneakers," Rita counseled. "The ones with Strawberry Shortcake are cute."

"For babies." Skeeter stuck out her lower lip, then tossed her head, pigtails bouncing. "I'm not going."

Rita cut her off. She squatted and locked gazes. "You have five minutes to get ready for Brett's game. If you don't, you'll lose TV privileges for the rest of the week. That's five long days, Skeets." Rising, she eyed the girl. "It's up to you."

In the old days she'd have wheedled the girl's cooperation, trying to assuage the guilt of Tom's crimes. She'd worked double time to make it up to them, be the nicest mom she could be, bending backward until she'd collapsed in an alcoholic heap.

Big mistake.

Unraveling two years of insanity wasn't easy, but doable now that she was sober. She stirred boiling water into an insulated jug containing hot chocolate mix. Sweet cocoa essence rose, rich and full, delighting her senses. If only she'd turned to chocolate instead of whiskey....

Her computer light blinked green from the quaint kitchen alcove, a reminder of Brooks' words. How could she find time to write up a professional prospectus with long hours of work and the intricacies of raising three children on her own, one of whom presented a constant challenge?

The phone rang. Rita grimaced, knowing her time frame was short. Her mother's phone number appeared in the display. Swallowing a sigh, Rita answered, one eye on the clock.

"You're home."

No exchange of pleasantries. No socially acceptable intro. Yup. That was Mom lately. "Hey, Mom, yes. I'm here. But Skeeter and I are on our way to Brett's soccer game."

"You've had supper already?" Critical doubt shaded her mother's words. Intentional? Maybe yes, maybe no. In either case Rita had a game to get to as long as Skeeter cooperated.

Please, Lord, let Skeeter cooperate tonight.

"Sandwiches later," Rita explained. Skeeter reappeared wearing the Strawberry Shortcake sneakers and an aggrieved expression. Rita nodded approval at one and ignored the other. Some things weren't worth the battle.

"How do kids get homework done when their schedules run them ragged day after day?" Judith Barnes' voice pitched higher. "Nothing should outrank homework. School performance. You above all people should know that, Rita. Your grades were excellent when you applied yourself."

In Mom-speak, that meant, "You didn't apply yourself often enough."

The ten seconds Skeeter had been kept waiting pushed her patience beyond endurance. She parked one hand on her hip and tapped a toe, the hint of bored insolence well practiced. At seven years old, it shouldn't be a consideration. With Skeeter it had become almost ingrained, not a good thing. "Um, hello? I thought we were going? Isn't that why I had to put these stupid shoes on?"

"I'm coming, Skeets." Rita added a silent frown, indicating displeasure at Skeeter's voice and tone. Skeeter rolled her eyes, her mouth curved down in a characteristic pout.

Great.

"Mom, I've got to go. Brett's game is going to start soon."

"Rita, you know I don't like to interfere—"

Rita knew nothing of the sort.

"And I generally mind my own business—"

Meaning I'm about to mind yours, so watch out….

"And I'm a firm believer in parents raising their own children—"

Translation: I could do better, hands down, no questions asked.

"But why do you let her talk to you that way? So bratty? Liv wasn't like that. Neither was Brett. But with Aleta you let her get away with all kinds of things you'd have never let slide before."

Before what? Tom's crimes? His suicide? Her alcoholism?

Her mother drew a breath, her voice a mix of concern, criticism and consternation, a gruesome threesome. "When she gets like that, she sounds just like her father. Proud and pretentious."

"Mom, I can't do this now. I have to go. Skeeter's waiting. So is Brett. I'll be glad to discuss my chronic failings at a later date, okay?"

"You don't have failings, Rita. You've made mistakes. Nothing the rest of us haven't done, myself included. I just don't want this to go too far, too long. It's hard to backtrack with kids."

Since Rita was fairly sure she'd let Skeeter's sour attitude grow out of control already, she couldn't say much in response. "I know, Mom. Gotta go. Talk to you later."

"All right."

Rita disconnected, checked her cell-phone charge because Liv would be calling later for a ride home, and nodded toward Skeeter's clothes and shoes as she twisted the top of the thermos.

"You look great." She raised the bright raspberry-toned bottle. "Hot chocolate for later."

Skeeter's eyes widened in appreciation.

"You might want to bring a book or stuff to color," Rita added. "If it gets really cold, you can sit in the car."

Rita moved aside to allow Skeets past. Stepping down, Skeeter caught her toe on a chipped porch tile. She crashed to her knees. Hysterical tears ensued, ruining the momentary peace. Rita leaned down, inspected both knees, grabbed the still-secure bottle and shrugged. "Not fatal. Let's go."

Skeeter glared.

Rita did a slow count to ten. She was segueing from eight to nine, weighing choices, when Skeeter stood, a martyred expression in place. Moaning, she limped to the door.

Obviously five days of no television loomed long and lonely. Rita took the positive-reinforcement route. "It'll make Brett happy to know we're at his game."

No answer. Ah, well. The sacrificial-lamb act would fade if ignored. After the day she'd had, Rita had no difficulty doing just that.

"Come on, Brett, that's it!" Rita fist-pumped as her son feinted right, dodged left, then sent the ball on a diagonal across the net where a teammate finished the play by tapping it in. Rita clapped and cheered with the rest of the Charger parents. The score was two–one with less than ten minutes to play. She turned as the teams regrouped and glanced at the parked car. The cold night made the backseat a welcome reprieve for Skeeter. Once they'd gotten to the field, she'd forgotten her snit and played with other sideline siblings until the damp air chilled them. Most of them had retreated to their respective cars as the temperatures dropped.

"Step by step," Rita reassured herself. It had taken time to plunge her family into the pits of despair, until a social services intervention spurred events that resulted in her sober state. Resuming an even keel wouldn't happen overnight.

"How's the game?" Brooks' voice startled her out of her reverie.

Rita's heart lurched. She frowned and turned, mad at her reaction, pretty sure half the single women in AA had a crush on Brooks at one time or another. His warm strength radiated solidity. She willed her pulse to calm and kept her voice even with effort. "We're winning. Brett just had an assist. That means he sent the ball to the player who kicked it in."

Brooks rocked back on his heels, one hand thrust into his pocket. His eyes crinkled. "I may not be a big fan but I comprehend the concept."

Embarrassed, she started to turn. He paused her action with a hand to her arm. "I brought you something."

He handed her a twenty-ounce convenience store cup. She eyed it, then him.

"Chai. The spiced variety. I thought you might appreciate a little warming."

She brought the cup to her nose and sniffed. Ah. Cinnamon. Vanilla. The undertone of mild tea. Rich cream. He watched her, head angled. "Since you wouldn't go out for tea, I thought the tea should come to you."

Warmth flooded Rita, and she hadn't even tried the tea.

"Dank night. You warm enough?"

And then some. Rita nodded, pulling her attention back to the game, not an easy task at the moment. "Fine, thank you. You're not at St. Luke's for the open meeting tonight?" Like several other venues, the quaint stone church on Windsor Street offered meeting space to AA members twice a week.

"Not tonight."

Rita refused to ponder the reasons that brought him here instead of there. Brooks had been in AA a long time. His years of sobriety and successful business acumen made him a standout example to others. If he could conquer the dragon of alcoholism, anyone could. He cocked his head and studied the growing fervor of the soccer contest, assessing. "Dangerous strategy. Gives the enemy too much time and latitude to perform."

"Enemy?" Rita's hiked brow questioned his word choice.

"I meant opponent," Brooks answered, not acknowledging the expression.

"But you said…"

He stopped her with a quieting look, classic Brooks. "The other team is about to score."

And they did.

A collective groan sounded. With scant minutes left, there

wasn't much chance of winning. Still, Brett's team had played a good game.

Rita drew a breath of clean, cold air, smiled and raised her cup. "Thank you, Brooks." She put the lid to her lips and sipped lightly, testing for temperature, then sighed her appreciation. "It's wonderful."

"Good." He watched as the teams offered the obligatory handshake before adding, "I got another compliment on your window today."

"Did you?"

"Yup. Customers from Vermont. They loved it. I was thinking you and Liv might be interested in doing a spring-summer version."

"Might be? We loved doing it. And I know Liv's got some ideas, she was just too shy to ask."

"Why?"

Rita shrugged. "She felt awkward, like she was pushing herself on you."

"She's got talent. An eye for color and balance that's inherent, not learned. Solid qualities."

"Thank you." Rita smiled up at him, his compliments sweet music to her ears. Liv had suffered from her parents' rough choices. As a result, she'd taken part in some escapades that had people wagging their tongues. But she'd turned a corner when Rita did. The thought of what her alcoholism had cost three wonderful kids gripped Rita internally.

That happened fairly often as memories stirred, but at least now she wasn't nearly as tempted to reach for a drink, a glass, a bottle. When she was, she handled those moments with help from Kim, Brooks and good old-fashioned faith. How she wished she'd turned to that first, but God had seemed pretty far removed after Tom's death.

"Earth to Rita?"

Rita flushed, caught in her thoughts. "Sorry. Thinking."

Brooks' look offered appraisal. "Remembering."

"Yes. How'd you know?"

"It shows all over your face."

"Great."

"Maybe just for me?" he suggested, an eyebrow up, his gaze steady and warm.

"That would be better than being an open book to the world at large. Half the county knows who I am and what I've done."

"Negative talk."

"Where I'd say realistic."

He weighed that. "County population was just over 100K in the last census."

She turned, exasperated. "You watch Jeopardy, don't you? I don't know another soul on the planet with such a head for random facts and figures."

"I'm a businessman," he corrected her, his voice matter-of-fact. "It's my job to know these things, to understand the shift in demographics and then adjust my sales strategies to fit."

"Enemies. Strategies." Rita took a step back, eyeing him, doing her own quick assessment. "You were a military man."

A flash of shadow darkened his features before he nodded. "For quite a while. Nice evaluation."

"Well, it's not like I haven't wondered," she confessed. Taking another sip of chai, she let the soothing mix warm her, the tea a great gift on a cold, clammy night. Her toes were chilled and she couldn't feel two fingers on her left hand, a leftover condition from childhood frostbite. But the warmth curled inside, way more satisfying than whiskey ever thought of being. And not nearly as scandalous. "You're a private person, Brooks. Everyone wonders."

"But no one asks."

"Reverting to my former statement: you're private. You like it that way. But you go out of your way to help others so they offer you respect in return."

"Ah." He rocked back on his heels, nodding. "In any case, I don't think fifty thousand people have a clue who you are or what you've done."

"I'll guarantee you one hundred percent know what Tom did."

"True enough," Brooks acknowledged, considering. Tom's

crimes had affected scores of local people. Despite its wide-spread geography, St. Lawrence County's population zones were centered in the towns and cities dotting Route 11, and big news like Tom Slocum's embezzlements made a notable splash in the headlines. With those numbers, everyone either knew or was related to someone affected by Tom's avarice.

The lack of insurance and the heavily mortgaged house had kept Rita right there in the midst of it all, her options limited by lack of finance and a downturn in the housing market, two tough smackdowns on top of the humiliation and grief. Her three kids lost their father, had to deal with the aftermath of his crimes and then watched their mother pitch downhill in the throes of alcoholism.

More than once he wished he could get his hands on Tom Slocum, give him the thrashing he so deeply deserved. What kind of man disregards his wife, his kids, to service his own greedy need?

"Hey."

Brooks shifted his jaw and his gaze. "Hmm?"

"I lost you."

"Must be contagious."

"I guess. Anyway, about the window? When should we do it?"

"Mondays are best. Weekends are too crazy to be pulling things out, playing with positioning and all that. This Monday maybe?"

"I'd have to bring Skeets," she warned.

"I'll alert the authorities. The police chief's right across the way and our three meager jail cells get precious little use. We'll be fine."

"Brooks."

He grinned.

"She's not that bad."

She was, and then some, but Brooks was a smart man. He had no intention of getting into the discussion now. He nodded toward Brett as he trotted off the field. "Fine game."

Brett shrugged, miffed by the loss. "Should have won it. We overkilled at the end and left them open."

"Recognizing that, you won't let it happen again."

"Exactly." Brett smiled his appreciation of Brooks' confidence.

"And you've developed a great left feint," Brooks went on. "The feint, followed by the fast feet, then dodge right... Well practiced. Great move."

Brett's smile deepened to a grin. "You played?"

Brooks shook his head. "I'm a baseball man. Not too many played soccer back in my day, but it wouldn't have mattered. I was born with a bat and ball in hand, according to my mother."

Brett's expression changed. "Were you named for Brooks Robinson?"

"Good connection," Brooks observed.

Rita noted his expression, a mix of surprise and chagrin.

"Not too many know that around here, but yes. My dad was an Orioles fan."

"Was? Oh. Sorry you lost him." Brett's look smacked of apology for bringing up a sore subject.

Brooks clapped a hand to the back of his head, bemused. Rita studied him, his reactions, his look. He drew a deep breath, exhaled and directed his answer to Brett. "He's not dead. I should have said *is* a big O's fan. We went to every Orioles game we could when I was a kid."

Another little tidbit of a past Brooks never talked about. *Interesting,* thought Rita.

"Mom!" Skeeter's pugnacious demand put a quick stop to her mental wanderings. The seven-year-old stomped their way, rude and discourteous. "I've been waiting forever and I'm cold and hungry and my brown crayon broke and I can't color a stupid tree without a brown crayon. What's taking so long? Stop talking and take me home. I hate it when you take so long!"

"Skeeter—"

Skeeter stomped her foot again, her normally cute features twisted.

Brooks took no pains to hide his assessment. He nodded Rita's way, ignored Skeeter, and said, "I'll see you soon, Reet. Brett, good game."

"Thanks, Mr. Harriman."

Rita started to stumble through a goodbye. Another foot stomp dragged her attention back to Skeeter as Brooks walked toward his truck.

Before her stood one very good reason why she couldn't entertain thoughts of a relationship. Not now. Probably not ever, at least not while she had to deal with Hurricane Skeeter on a daily basis.

Brett and Liv were old enough to appreciate the relative peace of Rita's sobriety and their current existence. Oh, she was still paying the price for stupidity, but things were better between them.

But Skeeter…

Not so much.

Frustrated, Rita headed toward the car at a quick clip, Skeeter following, her feet clomping in the cold, wet grass.

Which meant her shoes would still be wet for school tomorrow.

Another day, another confrontation.

Great.

Chapter Three

Rita sank into the comfy recliner, put her feet up and leaned her head back, relieved to call it a day. Had she really crawled out of bed eighteen hours ago, her 5:00 a.m. bakery start a distant memory now?

Liv poked her head around the corner. "Sitting down again?"

Rita laughed.

Liv took a seat across from her, her glance taking in the time. "Long day."

"For you, too."

Liv shrugged. "I got to spend my evening watching two cute kids, neither of whom yelled or screamed or stomped their feet." She jerked her head toward the upstairs, where Skeeter lay sleeping. "Got my homework done, studied for a chem test and watched cable, all while getting paid."

"Nice gig."

"It was." Liv stood and stretched, the day catching up with her. "But as much fun as it is watching the Bauers' kids from time to time, I want to get a real job."

Rita raised a brow. "What about sports? Running? After-school activities?"

"Lots of people juggle both," Liv answered. She rubbed her eyes, stretched once more and shrugged. "Something to think about. I hate making you chauffeur me around more than you already do, though. I know that's tough."

"It's no biggie, Liv. I'm your mom. That's what I do."

"But with our schedules all so different, it's not easy," Liv argued. "I just don't want to make things tougher."

Rita hesitated. Was Liv weighing this choice so heavily because she was afraid Rita would cave under pressure? She stood and hugged Liv's shoulder. "If you're ready for that step of independence, take it, kiddo. Seriously. You'll be sixteen in less than a year and then you can drive yourself places, at least some of the time. And you can become my part-time cabbie, tote your brother and sister all over for me."

Liv mock-scowled. "Great."

Rita grinned. "This could be a total win-win. I'm one hundred percent okay with that."

Liv's sigh of relief told Rita she'd nudged open a door for her daughter, curtailing her concerns.

Rita knew there were times when Brett and Liv held back, fear dogging their choices. Neither one wanted to be a catalyst in pushing her over an unseen edge, resulting in a fall off the wagon. With her one-year medallion safely tucked in her pocket, she wasn't quite as concerned as she used to be.

One day at a time. Sound advice.

"I'm heading to bed, Mom. You're off tomorrow?"

"Yes. Since it's my Saturday to work, I've got tomorrow to kick up my heels. Shop. Visit the spa. Do lunch."

Liv laughed. They both knew that Rita's scheduled day off meant playing catch-up on all the stuff back-burnered during the other six days of the week. Cleaning, laundry, shopping, errands, banking. The short hours between Skeeter's morning bus and afternoon bus were crammed full of tasks and chores needed to maintain some small vestige of normalcy.

And she just might outline her prospectus, push things forward. If she could hurdle this cycle of fear, of rejection, she could possibly plant herself into the dream job she'd hoped and planned for.

An image of the storefront in Canton filled her brain, her

creative side painting, trimming and polishing the scarred space into something warm, cozy and inviting, a respite from the long days of winter and the heat of the summer. A place to buy amazing pastries, cakes and cookies.

Did she dare put her mind to the test tomorrow? Give it a shot?

She yawned and realized she was too tired to make that decision now, but tomorrow...

Liv interrupted her musings. "Be sure to treat yourself to a nice massage once your nails are done."

Rita almost sighed. The very idea of a relaxing massage sounded absolutely wonderful and totally impossible. "I've decided pampering is overrated."

"And probably detrimental to womankind as a whole," Liv agreed. She hugged Rita one more time, understanding. "'Night, Mom."

"Good night, honey."

Rita turned out the lights as Liv's footsteps faded, the deepening shadows peaceful and quiet, a perfect contemplative time for prayerful thought and consideration.

Skeeter had settled down once they got home, probably too tired to battle it out. Rita hoped she'd wake in the morning in good humor, find something in her drawers that tickled her fancy, choose to wear the dry shoes they'd left at home tonight, have breakfast and get on the bus all smiles, like most sevenyear-olds.

Then return home tomorrow afternoon the same way.

Her gaze strayed to the kitchen where her computer lay dormant, its silence commanding attention.

Change the things you can...

Once Skeets was on the bus, Rita was tossing in the first load of laundry, starting the dishwasher and writing a prospectus. Once done, she'd have Brooks read it over, see if she'd covered all the bases. And then, applications.

Yeah, she could get knocked around emotionally, always a dicey thing for a recovering alcoholic. The chances of procuring the loan were slim.

But the chances went from slim to none if she did nothing, and that wasn't acceptable. Not anymore. She'd gotten braver and bolder in the past year. High time she took a chance. With her strengthening faith and the support of AA, she could take this step forward.

Fingering the bronze chip in her pocket, she nodded as she climbed the stairs. One day at a time.

Chapter Four

The metallic crash yanked Brooks from his bed later that night. Battle ready, one hand grabbed a weapon resembling a worn kitchen broom while the other sought the corner of the closed Venetian blind, his gaze searching the night.

A flash of red-gold skirted the pavement, enough to tell Brooks he'd been undermined by a four-footed varmint with a penchant for homemade mac and cheese.

Again.

He barreled toward the door wishing he'd remembered to turn the heat on after Brett's soccer game.

No.

Huffing against the cold, he grabbed the first thing his fingers hit, an old Baltimore Oriole's afghan. He yanked it around his shoulders and headed out the door, to no avail. Like previous times, the minute the door handle clicked left, the dog disappeared, obviously faster and smarter than Brooks.

Which didn't take much at 3:00 a.m.

Strewed garbage lay ankle deep across his small yard.

He bit back useless words, shook a fist, then danced sideways on the cold step, the chill of his feet knife-blading up, his outside thermometer reading twenty-nine degrees.

Brr…

And since his apartment wasn't much better, his living room offered little reprieve. Disgruntled, Brooks finagled a light, cranked the thermostat right, tugged on sweats and tried not to be upset that some scruffy dog had once again bested a decorated war veteran.

The drawer full of military medals offered small comfort as Brooks cleaned a frosted yard littered with disgusting debris. Why him? Why now? What was it about this garbage that drew the mutt repeatedly?

Probably your ineptitude to catch him, tweaked an inner voice.

Brooks couldn't disagree. Like it or not, the dog had bested him multiple times.

Resigned, Brooks did what he should have done days ago. He hauled the garbage tote into the garage and closed the door, then stared into the darkened night, his backyard melding into state forest land, the dog gone from sight but not from mind. "Next time, pal."

The promise of payback sounded thin. The dog was obviously smarter, quicker and sneakier.

And needed less sleep.

Brooks yawned, scowled, then headed inside. In one night he'd been bested by a cantankerous seven-year-old and a tenacious dog, both of which could use a lesson in manners. He eyed the clock, decided six hours was plenty of sleep, made coffee and headed to the wood shop, wondering why kids and dogs couldn't just behave themselves.

"Toots, did Hy Everts drop off those frames I ordered?" Brooks asked later that morning.

Tootsie Lawrence nodded as she hooked her deep green fleece in the workroom. "Late yesterday, actually. Do you have the picture Cade left? I'll frame it for you."

"Right here." Brooks handed an envelope to his longtime sales clerk. "The one with the blue matte is for Cade." The town's police chief had dropped off a family picture the week before.

"Beautiful." Tootsie withdrew the frame with care. Hy's work had become renowned, his wood carvings a natural expression of North Country life. The thick picture frames, a new venture for him, were engraved with north-woods symbols along the perimeter. Trees, bears, cabins, moose, wolves. The effect of the lighter wood recessed against the deeper stain held the pictures in relief. "Oh, Boss, look."

Brooks peered over her shoulder as Tootsie withdrew Cade's family picture, her expression beatific. "Isn't this just lovely?"

"You're crying."

"I'm not," Tootsie protested. She sniffled.

"You are," Brooks exclaimed, horrified. "Stop that. Now."

"I can't." Tootsie trailed a finger along the frame, her gaze trained on the sweet family before them. "And how cute is that baby, Boss?"

"Cute enough."

She swung around and offered him a stern expression. "He's absolutely, positively beautiful. Couldn't you just eat him up?"

Brooks couldn't, actually, but he knew better than to argue. Cade called just then, saving Brooks from himself. "Hey, Chief."

"Brooks, did my frame arrive yet?"

"We've got it. Tootsie's actually framing the picture as we speak."

"Sweet. Annie asked me about it and I promised I'd check. How does it look?"

Brooks eyed the framed print. Cade's young family laughed back at him. He swallowed a sigh, worked his jaw and nodded. "Very nice, which is a good thing since these frames don't come cheap."

"It doesn't matter," Cade told him. "As long as it's right, the cost is insignificant."

His words touched Brooks' heart.

Brooks was frugal. His lifestyle reflected that. He was constantly amazed at how quickly Rita went through money, week after week. Shoes here, doctors there, school supplies, car repairs, food, clothes. Her expenses boggled the mind.

Picturing Cade's family, Brooks realized he was the anomaly, not them. His singular status and prudence labeled him different.

Usually that didn't bother him.

Today it did.

A movement outside caught his attention, a flash of red-gold skirting the parking lot. "Cade, have you noticed this stray dog that's been hanging around?"

"No. How long's he been around?"

"Off and on for the last week or more," Brooks told him. He taped the edges and slid the frame into one of his distinctive cord-handled bags. "A retriever."

"Haven't seen him."

"I just caught a glimpse of him alongside the parking lot. He's been getting into my garbage at night, making quite a mess."

"Tags?"

"Haven't gotten close enough to see. He's furtive."

"Or smart."

"Either way, it's a pain to have to chase him off."

"I'll keep an eye out and let Bill Pickering know." Bill was the animal-control officer for St. Lawrence County.

The idea of the dog being caged niggled, but the thought of not having to wrestle garbage constantly won out. "Thanks." Brooks hesitated, then asked, "They won't put him down, will they?"

"That depends on a lot of factors," Cade explained. "If he's got an owner, tags, if he's healthy, adoptable. A lot of strays get put down. There are no guarantees."

"But he's not that bad," protested Brooks.

Cade went silent for a moment. When he spoke his voice held more than a hint of question and a good dose of amusement. "You either want him caught or you don't. Which is it?"

Brooks ran a frustrated hand through his hair and frowned. "I'm not sure, myself."

"Well, when you figure it out, call me back. I'm just across the road, so I'm fairly accessible."

"Thanks, Chief.

He wouldn't call, Brooks decided. The thought of the dog locked up in a pound bothered him. Not as much as the dog rummaging his garbage, but still…

Nothing to be euthanized for, right? A few scraps of paper, some old mac and cheese and one worn shoe that Brooks really should have tossed months ago.

Definitely not worth a death sentence, but Brooks couldn't deny he'd like to get a full night's sleep on a more regular basis, and hoped the locked-up garbage bin would ensure that.

Chapter Five

Rita took a deep breath, breathed a prayer for strength and dialed her brother-in-law Ed's home. "Heather, it's Rita. Is Ed available?"

Her former sister-in-law's voice faltered. "I'm not sure, Rita."

Rita sent her gaze upward, compressed her lips and bit back what she wanted to say. "I only need a minute."

"Who is it?" Ed's churlish voice came through gnarled, as if Heather tried to block the sensitive microphone a little too late.

"Rita."

"What does *she* want?" His emphasis on the pronoun smacked of disregard. Obviously Ed felt she had nothing to say that he wanted to hear. But if she was going to garner enough courage to run her own business and her own life, Rita needed to lasso some guts, take charge and do what was needed on a daily basis. A good businesswoman didn't put things off for her convenience or to shore up a sagging self-esteem.

"Tell him I need to talk to him, Heather. It's either talk to me now or I'll come right over."

"She says she's coming over if you don't talk to her."

Ed muttered words unsuitable for decent company and Rita hoped his kids were somewhere else. Anywhere else. But Ed's kids had been raised around his late-day vulgarity, the ever-present twelve-pack of beer an after-hours habit.

"What do you want?"

Rita heard his words and figured he was about six cans into the night and it was only five o'clock.

"Ed, you're aware the judge could make his decision any day regarding the pension fund, right?"

"I know you're trying to finagle your way into messing up my retirement fund, yes. And that any decent judge will see right through your little scheme and tell you to get your drunken butt out of bed and get a better job. Take care of my brother's kids."

His words hit their mark, but Rita choked back a retort. "Ed, if you split the fund now, I'll drop the case. I'm starting a bakery of my own and those funds would go a long way to helping me get on my feet."

"I'll tell you what," Ed expounded. "I know you're a worthless excuse for a wife and mother, that if Tommy hadn't been working night and day to keep you in fancy clothes and cars, he wouldn't have done what he did. You drove him to it, and we all know it."

"Ed, if you wait for the judge to rule, you could be liable for legal fees and court costs. Those add up."

"That judge ain't gonna give you a dime," Ed shot back. "You get your share when I get mine, at age sixty-five. That's how Tommy and I set it up, and that's how it is. Now leave me alone."

Click.

Rita stared at the phone, thinking of all the things she wished she could say, then sighed. Not one of them would change the outcome, change Ed's outlook or make a difference in the long run, so why say them?

Complete satisfaction?

Sure, yanking Ed's chain with a long-winded spiel might offer some sense of momentary comfort, but it was better she leave things be. She'd called, she'd tried, made an honest attempt. Now she'd go to the banks knowing she'd given it her best shot with Ed. Yeah, she'd come up short, but she hadn't chickened out or gone off on him. Two good things.

Having bank officers see her financial state of affairs unnerved her. Life hadn't been easy since Tom died and her drinking had messed the whole family up, but since she'd gone into recovery a year before, everything had been paid on time. That should count for something, right?

Maybe.

She pulled in another deep breath, turned her back on the phone and called Skeeter's name as she headed for the car.

"Liv? Skeets? You guys ready? We have to get to the wood shop."

"We're ready." Liv's light footsteps pattered down the stairs. Skeeter's followed at a more measured pace, but she wasn't testy, and Rita chalked that up as a quiet victory. "Do you need me to put anything in the car?"

"Nope. I did it while you were finishing your homework. Skeets, did you make progress on your room?"

Skeeter's expression said she hadn't.

Rita thrust up a brow. "This will come back to haunt you, kid. At some point you're going to ask to do something and I'll say, 'Is your room clean?'" Rita slanted her best mother-knows-everything look down to her youngest daughter. "And then you're going to be really mad at me and yourself for not getting it done like I've asked."

Choosing to let Skeeter stew on that, Rita climbed into the driver's seat, popped in a Taylor Swift CD, started the engine and headed toward North Country Woodcrafter, ready to immerse herself in creative expression. Sure, it was just painting whimsical wooden flowers to fit Liv's perceived motif for the spring-summer window, but she'd been looking forward to this all day.

Because you love seeing Brooks. You love it when he asks your opinion on fabrics, colors and stain tones or washes. He includes you and that makes you feel good.

It did, she realized. He sought her opinions, her ideas, as if her thoughts mattered.

Of course, he was like that with everyone, she assured herself, shutting down that twinge of inner knowledge. Brooks liked to help people in his quiet way, and he'd been a good friend and a patient listener since meeting her in AA. That was all she wanted or needed. A friend, a confidant. There was absolutely no way she was interested in anything more than that, not now, not ever, despite how his gray eyes crinkled in amusement when she was around.

Rita hadn't been accused of being amusing since about age eleven, and even then it was most likely accidental.

But Brooks laughed with her and at her, nudging her forward, fine-tuning her sense of humor. He wasn't afraid to spar with her, go toe-to-toe.

She wondered to herself why on earth that felt so marvelously good.

Once parked, Rita tugged the big plastic tub from the trunk of her car, balancing it on the trunk's lip as she juggled for a decent hand grip.

Strong arms descended around her, the scent of fresh-sawn wood and sweet oils tickling her nose.

Brooks. Smelling far too wonderful to ensure her peace of mind. A part of her longed to lean into the scent, the press of soft cotton knit comforting against her face.

He hoisted the tub from her hands, stepped back and surveyed it, then her. "You could ask for help, you know. It's not exactly a foreign concept."

"Why ask when I can do it myself?"

His frank expression offered more than his words. "Because I'm here? And available?"

Whoa. An opening too good to resist. Rita grinned. "I'll spread the word. Half the local singles will be dropping by with cookies and cakes, showing off their talents."

"I'll let that pass," Brooks told her. He grinned at Liv as she came around the side of the car, Skeeter's hand clutched in hers. "Ladies' night, hmm?"

Liv smiled up at him. "Yup. And Tootsie's hanging out with us. Skeeter's our gopher. What we need, she gets."

To Rita's relief, Skeeter smiled. She saw Brooks note that, and was pretty sure the big guy breathed a sigh of relief. She knew she did. "Liv, if you and Skeeter can get the door, I've got the grass mat to get."

"Grass mat?" Brooks rearranged the tub to a more comfortable position and hiked a brow. "For?"

"You'll see," Rita promised. She hauled the folded mat from the backseat and headed inside. "We're about to welcome spring full force at North Country Woodcrafter."

"I see."

She ignored the twinge of concern in his tone. Brooks didn't hand over the reins often or well. Better he should go to a meeting or work in the wood shop or in the clean room or anyplace other than the showroom while they broke down the winter display and replaced it with Liv's creativity. Having him on hand would make her the tiniest bit crazy. Just before they got to the door, Rita did an about-face. "Head in with that, Brooks. I forgot something."

She hurried back to the car, swung open the front passenger-side door, reached down and grabbed the folder she'd brought for his approval.

Her prospectus, the layout of her bakery. Clutched in her right hand lay the career dreams and aspirations she'd kept on hold for years.

Would he laugh at it? Criticize? Advise?

She wasn't sure. It had been a lot of years since her business classes at SUNY Albany, but Rita understood the basic concepts as well as anyone. Exercise minimal risk to the maximum financial advantage. Guard the pennies, the dollars will come. Sage advice.

Brooks met her as she pushed through the entrance door. He took the mat from her hands, frowned as if thinking too hard, then shrugged. "I'm getting pizza later for everyone. Seven-thirty good?"

Rita surveyed the window, measuring time and space. "That gives us two hours. We should be fine. If not, we'll finish before the meeting at St. Luke's tomorrow."

Brooks shook his head. "I can't ask you to give up two nights in a row. I know how crazy your schedule is, Reet."

She waved a hand, already unpacking the tub, setting things out, giving Liv an overall view of what they had to work with. "You didn't ask, I offered. Whole different thing. And Liv and I don't do half-baked, Brooks. Really, you should know that by now."

"And here's more stuff," offered Tootsie as she entered from the wood-shop area, her arms full. "These are things we've used in the past."

"I'm totally loving the wooden flowers," exclaimed Liv. She stepped back, hair swinging, head tilted in a manner much like Rita's despite their dissimilar coloring, and nodded. "Skeets, can you help Tootsie carry the stuff that was in the window to the back room please?"

"Sure."

Brooks almost choked. He stared at the little girl, wondering who had taken over her body in the past thirty-six hours, then realized the truth with a full-fledged *thunk*. Skeeter Slocum had been taken over by a pod person.

All Brooks really knew was that the sweet, smiling kid in front of him offered a welcome respite from her usual prickly nature.

"Brooks, you need to leave," Rita instructed.

A part of Brooks loved seeing her take charge, get a little bit bossy. Another part fought for total control. He subdued that with effort. "Where would you suggest I go?"

Rita laughed. "Sorry, I didn't mean it that way. It's just that we want to surprise you and if you're here, I'm going to second-guess myself, which will just annoy Liv. So we're better off if you work out back. That way if we have questions, you're available—"

"But not in the way."

"Exactly." She beamed up at him, tiny laugh lines crinkling the corners of her pretty blue eyes. A wisp of hair fell across her face as she turned, a tiny strand, just big enough to make him want to reach out, smooth it back.

So he did.

The warm expression his touch inspired threw him off guard. Eyes wide, her look swept up, met his, a flash of awareness ping-ponging between them until he broke the connection by dropping his hand. Stepping back.

She breathed deep, in relief or consternation, maybe a combination of the two, then thrust something into his hand. "If you have time, will you read this over? See if it makes sense from a business standpoint and has all the information a loan officer would need?"

Brooks recognized what he held. He smiled in approval, nodded and tried to pretend the whole sparks thing was a glitch. "You did it."

"I did," she admitted. She dropped her gaze to the folder, then brought it back to him. "I think it's good."

"Then I'm sure it is, but I'd be glad to go over it, offer advice if needed."

"Thank you, Brooks."

Her grateful smile melted another chink in his self-imposed armor. He hesitated, wanting to say more, then noticed Liv, Tootsie and Skeeter were all staring at them.

Time to go.

He held the prospectus up, nodded and headed out back. "I'll be back here until the pizza comes."

"Pizza?" Tootsie turned toward Rita and Liv as Brooks disappeared into the workrooms.

"Brooks is ordering some for later. Around seven-thirty. And we should be almost done by then."

Tootsie paled. Her throat convulsed.

Rita angled her head, concerned. "You okay, Toots? You're not still sick, are you?"

"I'm fine."

Her words were less than convincing, but Rita understood the need for privacy. She nodded. "Okay, Liv, take it away. What's first?"

"I need Skeeter to line up all the flowers and wooden animals we have so I can get an idea of height and balance," Liv instructed.

Rita smiled inside. Liv was a born creator, and this task would keep Skeeter busy for a while and feel as if she was contributing. Great combination.

"And, Mom, I'm going to reverse-paint window images so that they appear to be moving forward from the outside vantage point. That's going to take me a while, so if you and Tootsie could paint those flowers there, using bright summer tones, by the time they're dry I should be able to lay the grass mat behind the painted grass stems."

"Got it." Rita handed Tootsie a brush. "If we do this in the clean room, we're out of the way and have more space to work."

"Perfect," Toots agreed.

"You girls are okay out here?" Rita hiked a brow to Liv.

"A-okay." Liv sent Skeeter a reassuring grin. "With Skeets' help I can get this done fairly quickly. Right, Skeets?"

"Right."

Rita blessed whatever combination had resulted in a non-combative evening, but was wise enough to keep her comments to herself. "We'll be right back here if you need us."

"Thanks, Mom."

Rita grinned at Skeeter, her earnest expression warm and sincere. This was the kid she'd like to see on a more regular basis. Maybe her strategies were working at long last, but Rita had been Skeeter's mother for a long time. She wouldn't be banking on it. Not yet, anyway.

Chapter Six

"This is wonderful, Rita."

Brooks' voice jerked Rita out of her work zone. Her brush slipped and scarlet paint daubed his benchtop, the bright tone a standout against the clear, sealed wood. "Oops."

His easy grin reassured her. "That's why everything here is washable. Total necessity."

His gaze canvassed the painted flowers, perky in their newly enameled finish. "Great effect already."

Tootsie nodded. "Isn't it, Boss? Talk about eye-catching."

"As if you needed to catch any more business." Rita made the observation as she used a fine-tipped brush to accentuate stem and leaf definition. "This place is hopping on a regular basis."

"More business is never a bad thing." Brooks held up her prospectus. "As you pointed out here. This is excellent, Reet."

"Really?" Warmth spread through her, inspired by that heart-stopping smile.

But Rita had already made ginormous mistakes in the happily-ever-after department, and even though Brooks was a wonderful guy who would be Mr. Right for someone, he held himself just a little apart.

So had Tom.

Brooks liked his solitude.

So had Tom.

Rita had let herself be fooled by Tom's charm, his brains, his charisma. She'd taken second place to his work, his fun and games, and then his embezzlement schemes.

Nope, she wasn't looking for romance, not now. Her current efforts were best concentrated on raising her kids, keeping a semblance of order at home and striving to start a new business. That alone made her way too busy to contemplate silly things like fairy-tale endings with a guy who refused to darken the door of a church. While privacy wasn't a bad thing, Brooks' need for solitude sent warning signs flashing Do Not Enter!

"There are a couple of points I'd elaborate on a little more."

"Such as?"

Brooks angled his chin toward their current project. "Let's not discuss it now. Tomorrow night maybe? After the meeting? You've got Wednesday off, right?"

She did, but was surprised he remembered since her schedule changed weekly. Surprised and more than a little pleased. "Yes."

"Then let's talk about it after fellowship," he suggested, his gray eyes thoughtful. "Have you considered where to apply?"

"I have. I'll bring the list with me and we can go over it together."

"Good." He hesitated, his look saying he'd like to linger, his body language saying something else, although with a reluctance Rita didn't often see. "I'll head back to the workroom."

Ah. He wanted to stay, be part of the action. Or maybe direct the action...

No, Rita decided, he just wanted to join in. Work with them. "Bunnies are next on our agenda. You ever painted a bunny, Brooks?"

Did he pale under that weathered skin?

"You're kidding, right? Rabbits in my window? With the flowers?"

Rita shared a grin with Tootsie. "And birds," Tootsie quipped. "You've read *Bambi,* Boss, right? All the little forest creatures hopping about, twitterpated."

"Twitter-what? Never mind." Brooks ran a big blunt hand through his hair and finished the action by rubbing the back of his neck, his face bemused. "You know where I am if you need me."

Rita slanted a grin up to him.

The action stopped him. He contemplated her, his gaze a mix of rough and tender, sweet and strong, his eyes warming at her smile before he pulled himself away. He turned back at the door linking the clean room to the workroom. "Pepperoni and sausage?"

"Yum."

Tootsie nodded, kind of, but Brooks didn't catch her hesitation.

Rita did.

When Brooks had disappeared into his work area, Rita laid a hand along Tootsie's arm. "What's going on, Toots?"

"Nothing. Why?"

"Are you still feeling sick?"

"I'm fine."

Her ducked chin told Rita otherwise. "You're not. Have you seen a doctor? Seriously, honey, this has been going on too long. You've been sick off and on for the better part of a month."

Tootsie swallowed hard, eyes down, then sighed. She averted her gaze, staring at nothing, then dragged her gaze back and met Rita's eyes. "I saw Dr. Renson last week."

One of the area's busiest and most sought-after obstetricians.

Rita drew a breath, worked her jaw and reached out to clasp Tootsie's hands. "When is the baby due?"

"December."

"A Christmas baby." Rita beamed, trying to lighten the moment, soften the situation. "The time for miracles, Toots."

A tiny smile softened Tootsie's worried features, but just for a moment. Worry redescended, pushing Rita to grab her in a hug. "It'll be fine, honey. I promise. Does Matt know?"

Matt was Tootsie's soldier fiancé, currently deployed to Iraq.

"No."

"You haven't told him?"

Tootsie paled. "No."

"But why?" Rita wondered out loud, confused. "Toots, you're engaged, it's not the end of the world. Why haven't you told him?"

Tootsie drew in a deep breath and straightened her shoulders. "Because Matt hasn't been home since last Thanksgiving."

It didn't take a rocket scientist to do the math. Rita sank back in her chair. "Oh, no."

"Exactly." Tears pooled in Tootsie's bright brown eyes, their cinnamon tone matching hair of similar color, such a pretty combination. "I don't know how to tell him what I've done. I'm so ashamed."

"Does Brooks know?"

Tootsie shook her head. "Absolutely not. Brooks is a good guy and a stellar boss, but he's a staunch conservative and big on faith and following the rules. He'd never understand how I could do such a thing."

Rita shifted forward, concerned. "Tootsie, nothing is unforgivable. Do you remember the gospel story about the adulteress? How the Pharisees sentenced her to be stoned?"

Tootsie drew back, remorse twisting her features.

Rita gripped her hands and leaned forward. "Jesus told the crowd that those without sin should cast the first stone. And slowly, one by one, they dropped their stones and walked away because we're all sinners, honey. Each and every one of us. And God forgives those sins. All we have to do is ask." She gave Tootsie's hands an encouraging squeeze, hoping her empathy rang true. "Things happen, Toots. God knows that. And you've got friends nearby, people who will stand by you. Help you."

"No family."

"We'll be your family," Rita insisted. Tootsie had been raised by a live-off-the-land aunt in a smaller-than-small town near Malone, but her aunt had moved to Arizona several years ago, leaving Tootsie dating Matt and working for Brooks. This new turn of events would most likely sever Tootsie's ties to

Matt's family, leaving her abandoned. "You've got us, kiddo. I promise."

Tootsie's jaw quivered. She firmed it, straightened and set her shoulders back, determined. "It'll be fine, I know. Eventually. I just dread telling Matt. And Brooks."

"If you need me around when you do it, I'll be glad to ride shotgun."

"Planning a bank heist?" Liv crossed the room smiling, one brow hiked as she surveyed the bright promise of their painting efforts. A glimpse of Tootsie's tear-streaked face blotted out her smile. "Toots, what's up?"

Tootsie waved her away. "It's nothing, I'm fine."

Liv rolled her eyes. "Yeah and Gretzky's just another hockey player."

"Your mom can tell you later. Right now—" Tootsie repositioned herself, chin down, eyes on the first bunny "—I need to work."

"All right." Liv stepped back, worry shading her brow. A tiny head shake from Rita erased the frown. "These are perfect," she exclaimed, eyeing the finished flowers. "Skeeter is helping me lay the matting. The glass images are done and drying. We actually might be able to get this done tonight."

"Bunnies won't be dry," Rita warned her.

"That's no big deal." Liv shrugged. "Toots can put them in place tomorrow. The flowers and the window art were the biggies. I've just got to have Brooks approve what's done so far."

"Approval granted."

Brooks' deep voice drew their attention to the door. He nodded to Liv, pleased. "It looks wonderful, Liv."

She colored at the praise. "Really? You like it?"

His expression underscored his words. "I love it. You're one talented young lady. And working in reverse like that? That's a rare ability few artists possess."

Her blush deepened. "Thanks, Mr. Harriman."

"Brooks," he corrected her. "If you ever want a job, kid, come see me first."

Liv raised her chin, surprise and pleasure vying for her features. "Seriously?"

"Honey, my offers are never less than serious."

"That's for sure," quipped Rita. She watched the exchange between Brooks and Liv, her heart tripping just a little bit faster.

Liv respected Brooks. It was obvious in her manner, her attentiveness, her awareness of detail in his presence. Something about him inspired others to reach a little higher, go a little faster, try a little harder, that indiscriminate quality that screamed leadership in calm undertones.

Brooks slid his gaze to Rita's, offered her a half smile that made her heart pump faster than normal, then returned his attention to Liv. "You say the word, kid. You're hired."

"Mom?"

Liv turned toward Rita.

Rita sat back on her stool, worked her jaw, then eyed them both. "She's been wanting to get a job," she explained to Brooks, her gaze shifting from him to Liv and back. "And I can't think of any place I'd rather have you work than here."

Brooks smiled.

Liv whooped. "Really, Mom? You don't mind?"

Brooks raised a hand of caution. "You still need to help your mother with Skeeter."

"And keep your grades up." Not that grades were a problem with Liv, not since Rita had reinstated herself as the mother, relieving Liv of responsibility. Liv had endured a couple of tough years, but she seemed determined to move on with her life, taking charge of her dreams. At fifteen, her attitude was pretty remarkable after what she'd gone through.

"Can we work around that?"

"Absolutely." Brooks arched a brow and indicated the showroom with a slight jerk of his head. "If I have you here to help Tootsie and Ava on the sales floor while learning cool things about fine carpentry on the side, I think we've got a deal, kid."

"And Ava will love not being dragged in for extra shifts,"

Toots noted. "She loves being here but with two little kids, she only has so much time. When we're crazy busy it definitely takes a crew on the sales floor."

Liv's hug surprised Brooks. Rita saw it in his face, his eyes, the girl's embrace taking him aback before he returned it. He winked at Rita over Liv's head. "I get artwork from this one and cookies from you. I love knowing your family, Reet."

His light words inspired her smile. "Well, we like you, too, and while all this chitchat is fun, it's not exactly getting the job done. I've got to get Skeeter home for bed in just a little bit."

Skeeter.

In all this time, everyone had forgotten that Skeeter was alone in the store.

A crash of something breakable and most likely valuable fixed that.

Liv and the three adults crowded through the door to the showroom. Scattered pieces of a vase lay shattered on the floor, remnants of dried flowers strewn among the broken pottery. Skeets' face wore a mix of fear and belligerence, not a pretty combination. "It was an accident."

Liv stepped in first. "Skeeter, it's all right, I'll pay for it. I shouldn't have left you alone out here."

"I'm fine alone. There's too much stuff all over the place is all."

Her tone said they were treading dangerous ground, never a good thing.

"But you weren't supposed to touch things, Skeet." Rita stood her ground, not wanting the situation to fly out of control but unwilling to downplay Skeeter's responsibility.

"I didn't," she protested, her hands flying up. "I was just backing up and knocked into the stupid thing. Everything's in the way here."

Rita colored, embarrassed.

Brooks grabbed a short broom and dustpan from behind the counter. "It is close in here," he told Skeeter. He handed her the dustpan. "If I sweep this up, can you hold this for me?"

She swept him a look of disdain. "I'm not a baby."

"Then stop acting like one," Liv told her. "You were supposed to stay by the window and arrange the birds."

"You were taking too long."

Rita couldn't argue with that. Skeeter wasn't exactly the kind of kid you trusted in a shop full of stuff on her own. Her fault, she knew.

"Hold the dustpan for Mr. Harriman and apologize."

Skeeter glared at her mother, then Liv.

A young man with a large pizza box stepped in the main door. "Your pizza, sir?"

Brooks nodded toward the cash-register counter. "Money's right there in an envelope."

The young man nodded.

Toots accepted the pizza, the teasing scent reminding them supper was at hand.

Rita hoped the smell of food would break Skeeter's standoff.

Nope.

"I'm not cleaning it up with him." Her look said she had sized Brooks up and recognized a foe.

"Then clean it up on your own." Brooks handed her the broom. "We're eating."

Dangerous move. Rita watched as Brooks followed Tootsie out back, the scent of fresh-baked, thick-crust pizza assailing their senses.

Liv eyed Skeeter and the mess. "I'll help since I'm the one who left you alone."

Rita hesitated, wanting to push Brooks' point and make Skeeter clean up the mess herself since she rejected his help so rudely, but wanting peace, as well. A full-blown Skeeter attack in the wood shop would not be pretty.

"That's nice of you, Liv."

"It's just a stupid old jar," Skeets sputtered. She pushed the broom toward Liv grudgingly. "He's got too much junk here."

Her comment brought Liv's back up. She straightened and eyed her little sister. "It's not junk."

"Whatever."

Liv's hazel eyes went smoke-toned in a heartbeat. "Don't 'whatever' me, Skeets. You weren't supposed to be anywhere near this table or this vase and I offered to help you because I felt bad for leaving you alone and because Brooks is a real good guy for letting us do this stuff." Liv took two steps forward, her body language offering a stern warning to errant little girls.

Like Skeeter cared.

"You don't 'diss' what Brooks has in here. Got it?"

Skeeter met the stare-down one-on-one, either brave or fool-hardy. "I don't care what he has. I want to go home. I hate this place."

"Skeets, let's get this done," Rita interjected. "Come on. I'll sweep. You hold the dustpan."

"No."

"You'd prefer to wait in the car?"

"I'd prefer to go home. Now."

"That's not an option." Liv stood her ground, gaze set, eyes fuming. "Brooks let us work here, ordered us pizza and just gave me a job. We're staying."

"I'm not." Skeeter whirled and flounced toward the door.

Rita caught her arm. "Do you want to go without TV and treats the rest of the week?"

"N...no."

"Then rethink your choices."

The lower lip thrust out, a sure signal of Hurricane Skeeter making landfall.

She ballyhooed at the top of her voice, shouting the injustice of Brooks, her mother, Liv and life in general.

Liv glared.

Rita prayed.

Skeeter yelled.

"The police station's right across the street." Brooks reentered the room looking partly annoyed and partly helpless, an unusual combination. "Cade showed me where he hangs the keys to the empty cells. She'd be safe and we could eat in peace."

Tempting offer but... "I'll take her home."

Brooks moved forward, ignoring Skeeter, which wasn't easy considering her volume. "That's not fair to you and Liv."

"Well, life isn't always fair, Brooks." Rita knew that first-hand, didn't she? Hadn't she tried everything under the sun to keep Tom happy? In the end, it wasn't enough. In retrospect, she knew nothing would have been enough to appease Tom's hunger for power, greed for money and prominence. Oh, he'd played the part well, a showman all the way, his weekly presence at church service a sham that covered the heart of a cheat and embezzler.

Outwardly he shone like a gleaming jewel, a salesman to the max.

And she'd been fooled, like all the rest, at least to a certain degree. That was almost as embarrassing as it was shameful. Some suspected she'd been part of his schemes, his deceit.

Nope. Just clueless. A part of her thought that might be even worse than being complicit. At least complicity indicated intelligence.

"I'll drop her off, get her settled and come back for Liv."

"I can bring Liv home."

Brooks looked less than pleased by her plan. Oh, well.

"Thanks, but no. I'll come back. My kid, my job."

Brooks looked about to argue the point, then didn't. He stepped back, shot Skeeter a look that indicated a preference for strong-arm tactics mixed with relief that Rita was handling her, then shrugged. "I'll see you at the meeting tomorrow."

"Right."

Her stomach growled, the scent of hot pizza a reminder of a hectic day and a long time since her last meal.

Skeeter flounced through the door, stomped her way to the car and shoved her way through Liv's supplies to climb into the backseat.

She was a brat, plain and simple.

God, help me. I'm in over my head with this one, and she's adept at picking the world's worst places for her tantrums and tirades. Show me what to do, how to handle her. Help me be strong when a really big part of me just wants her to be quiet. And nice.

Change the things you can...

Her catchphrase of the day, the month, the year.

Skeeter was her responsibility, her job, her child. It was up to Rita to fix the problem, one way or another.

As she passed the small Grasse Bend police station, Brooks' words came to mind. Hmm, jail cells for seven-year-olds?

Definite potential if she didn't get this obnoxious behavior under control, the sooner the better.

The thought of her hard-worked prospectus inspired a wince. How could she even contemplate an undertaking of that magnitude if she couldn't gain enough of Skeeter's cooperation to help with a simple thing like Brooks' front window?

Right now, with Skeeter sulking and sputtering in the backseat, she had no idea.

Chapter Seven

"Steve, this is Brooks Harriman. I'm standing on Main Street in Canton, looking at a vacant storefront next to Higby's Hardware. What can you tell me about it?"

"I'll show you instead," Steve answered. Steve had brokered real-estate deals throughout the region for over two decades. Better than most politicians, Steve Laraby knew the North Country, the people, the places, the mixed demographic that drew Brooks north over a decade ago. "I'm just up the road. Be there in five."

"I'll wait."

Brooks passed the time surveying the town's quaint Main Street. With the beautiful and historic campus of St. Lawrence University jutting off from the right, the town-square park and the redbrick storefronts offered the feel of yesterday in a town gearing for today. Electronics stores muscled in alongside quaint storefronts holding law offices, a small restaurant, a CPA, two insurance offices and a host of other small businesses.

No bakery. Nothing even resembling a bakery or bakeshop-slash-coffeehouse.

"Steve." Brooks shook Steve's hand once the Realtor stepped onto the sidewalk. He jutted his chin north. "Have people been using the state funds for storefront refurbishing?" The village of Canton had received generous grant monies to encourage a needed face-lift on some of the town's historic buildings. When

St. Lawrence County's manufacturing class shifted overseas, the downturn in population and money resulted in wear and tear throughout the area. Less money to pay bills meant even less spent on amenities.

"Most of the qualifying buildings have used funds," Steve told him. "But there's still a chunk for the asking and if it doesn't get used up, the state will rescind it in January. A lot of people hate the paperwork process involved."

Brooks eyed the vacant storefront before them. "This building qualifies?"

Steve nodded. "Definitely. But Horace Tompkins owns it and he's not of a mind to monkey with paperwork, in his words."

Brooks grinned. "That sounds like Horace. I'll swing by his way, offer my help."

"Good luck on that. I offered and he nearly chewed my head off, spouting something about danged city slickers botherin' him night and day."

Brooks shrugged. "He's a marine. He'll talk to me."

Steve sent Brooks an appraising look and nodded. "Everybody does, Brooks. For a quiet man, you attract a following."

Brooks shrugged that off.

He didn't want a following. He'd spent a long time leading, commanding, trekking with men into battle. Now he just wanted peace. Quiet. Sanctity.

Skeeter's tantrum the previous night had sent him a gut punch. How was Rita going to handle a new business venture when she couldn't count on the kid to behave herself for an hour?

"May I ask what you're considering this for, Brooks? You opening a Canton site for your furniture business?"

Brooks laughed and shook his head. "Keep overhead minimal and cash flow maximum. No, I'm happy in Grasse Bend, pulling from local markets and the tourist trade. And the university draw."

Steve nodded in the direction of St. Lawrence's campus. "Huge, for sure, if the product invites expenditure. And yours does. So." He paused and looked around the store. "What are you thinking? If you're free to tell me, that is."

"I have a friend interested in this site," Brooks explained.

Steve's interest spiked a grin. "Rita Slocum?"

"Yes." Brooks met his gaze. "You know Rita's interested in this location?"

Steve nodded, then directed Brooks to the back of the store. "We went over it inch by inch. I tried to fudge a few things, fluff them off, and she nabbed me on every one. Smart girl you've got there."

Brooks grinned, thought of setting Steve straight, then realized too much protest only added fuel to the rumor mill. "Rita's got a great head on her shoulders."

Steve barked out a laugh. "If that's all you've noticed, Brooks, you're more than a little hardened. The woman's beautiful."

Brooks straightened, chin raised, his shoulders broad and blunt, remembering Steve's marriage had dissolved nearly two years before. That made him single and in his mid-forties, just a tad older than Brooks. "I'd noticed."

"Ah." Steve nodded, respectful. "I thought as much. It would be hard not to."

"Right now she's interested in opening a business." Brooks wasn't sure if he was trying to convince Steve or himself. Maybe both. "And I want to help her."

"Understandable."

"It is," Brooks agreed. "No one bakes like Rita."

Steve nodded, but the spark of light in his dark eyes told Brooks he wasn't completely buying Brooks' business interest. Neither was Brooks, but the Realtor didn't have to know that.

"And she'd looked at a location in Grasse Bend, but this one offers her the university crowd nine months of the year."

"And the tourism crowd the other three. Six, actually, with the influx of people 'seeing the leaves' in the fall." Steve pointed out the angled back wall. "Years ago, Horace bought this back section from Bob Higby's father to help him out of a jam, so this section is actually directly behind Higby's store. The increase in square footage included extra parking."

"And higher taxes."

"We could try arguing them down," said Steve.

"Good idea. Let's fill out a purchase offer, run it by my lawyer, then present it to Horace."

Steve's eyes brightened at the unexpected request. "Now? Full asking price?"

"Right now and yes. You don't juke a marine, not when the price is fair. I've got to get back to work in time for Mick's lunch. Call me later, let me know if all's well. Instead of seeing Horace about grant applications, I'll fill them out myself and we can postdate them. I need closing to be fast so I can start renovation work, say by the first of next week?"

"Any financing involved?"

"Cash."

Steve's smile spread wider. "I love cash."

Brooks met his grin and relaxed into a smile of his own. "I thought you would."

The phone rang as Rita finished her list of facts and figures later that afternoon. She noted the caller ID, cringed and sighed. "Hey, Mom."

"I'm calling to remind you about your father's birthday on Tuesday. You should call him or at least send him a card this year."

Keep the peace, Rita. It's so not worth the fight. "I sent out a card this morning, actually, but I'll call, too. How's Dad doing?"

"For a man who's given his life for his kids and has one in the midst of a messy divorce and the other one a widowed alcoholic, I'd say he's getting by."

"Have you heard from Michael?" Rita's younger brother's troubled marriage had been on the edge of collapse for several years, but her mother still feigned surprise over the divorce petition his wife instituted.

"Michael tends to his own affairs."

Meaning Michael didn't call to get reamed out on a regular basis. Rita couldn't say she blamed him. She drew in a deep breath. "Mom, I've got to go. I've got some work to finish up here before I meet a friend tonight."

"What friend?"

One, two, three, four…

Counting to ten wouldn't cut it, not with Mom, and Rita didn't have the time or inclination to go to triple digits. "I'm working up a business plan to open my own bakery."

"You're what?"

From Judith Barnes' tone you'd have thought Rita just announced plans to instigate global warfare or wear white shoes after Labor Day, equally heinous crimes in her world.

"I'm drawing up a plan to open my own bakery."

"With three kids? One of whom is a perfect brat? Mark my words, Rita, that one is trouble, a chip off the old block, just like her father. A Slocum through and through."

That scorched.

"We're not discussing this, Mom. Skeeter's my problem, not yours."

"And a problem she is," declared Judith. "She needs a firm hand and a good spanking if you ask me."

"I didn't ask."

"More's the pity. Your father and I would never have tolerated such behaviors, but then we worked hard to be the kind of role models children looked up to."

"Mom, I totally get that you're disappointed in me, my life, my children and my existence on the planet, but I think it's in everyone's best interests if we move beyond the drama, okay? I haven't got the time to go there with you anymore. What's done is done. I'm not moving backward and I wish you'd move beyond it, too."

"Well, I—"

Rita cut to the chase. "I have to go. I can't be late for tonight's meeting. I'll talk to you soon, but I meant what I said, Mom. It's time to move on."

She hung up the phone and turned.

Skeeter stood there, her expression hard, her eyes cool. "That was Grandma?"

Rita choked back the sigh. "Yes."

"She doesn't like me."

Rita crouched down. "She loves you. She's your Grandma. She just gets crotchety sometimes."

Skeeter sent her a look of appraisal mixed with disbelief. "Whatever you say, Mom."

First her mother, now Skeeter. Rita thought hard, weighing her choices, then waded in. "Grandma's got her own way of doing things. She doesn't like change and when things do change, it bothers her."

"That's what makes her mean?"

"Not mean, exactly..." Truth prickled Rita. Her mother did seem mean sometimes, especially lately. Was it good to pretend otherwise, to deny it? "Well, yes, sometimes she's mean when she gets angry. But she's not always like that."

"I don't remember her ever being different."

Good point. At seven years old, Skeeter had experienced little normalcy in her life up to last year. Tom's scheme had come undone when she was still a toddler. Since then she'd had to deal with the confusion surrounding his downfall, his suicide, Rita's drunkenness and having to live with her aunt Sarah while Rita got her act together.

The poor kid had nothing but perpetual disturbance to fall back on. None of the good memories of early childhood, like Brett and Liv had, of Rita baking, throwing birthday parties, getting them involved in community activities from an early age. Swimming, dance, soccer, T-ball.

Yup. She'd messed this one up big-time, just like her mother said. And the idea of fixing it, getting things right?

Mind-boggling.

"How's your room?"

A fleeting look of dismay darkened Skeeter's features. "I'm too tired."

After her mother's dressing down and her own internal realization of how she'd thoroughly worked this kid over, Rita was tempted to placate her, try to make things up to her by cushioning her life from his point forward.

A stern voice challenged from within. *Change the things you can. Two wrongs don't make a right.*

"Well, free time becomes nonexistent for kids who refuse to follow the rules. Your room is your responsibility, Skeet. Not mine."

"I don't care if it's messy."

"I do. And since I bear the brunt of your attitude whenever you can't find something you want or need because it's buried on the floor, or under the bed, or in the back of your closet…"

Skeeter flushed, Rita's words hitting their mark.

"It becomes my problem."

"I know where everything is."

She didn't, Rita knew that from the expression on Skeeter's face, but she shrugged that off. "You've already lost treats and TV for the week because of your behavior last night."

The flush deepened, but Skeeter stayed quiet, probably hoping for a stay of execution. Rita was in no mood to offer pardons.

"I'll just add that you're grounded until that bedroom shines."

"But—"

"No buts. No extra chances. No wheedling or whining. Get your room done and we'll go from there. End of discussion."

Rita left Skeeter looking bemused and belligerent. As she started the car, she prayed for Liv's patience, but refused to miss tonight's meeting to mollify Skeeter. She had her cell phone with her and the church was only short minutes away. If Liv needed her, she'd call.

Was Rita a really bad mother for hoping that wouldn't be necessary?

She hoped not.

Chapter Eight

The cool glow of overhead fluorescents danced pale gold highlights off Rita's hair as she stepped into the basement meeting room at St. Luke's that night. The thin light warmed as it bathed her, the gold knit of her pullover sparking metallic points of radiance when she moved. Simply put, she looked beautiful, the slim gold chain around her neck complementing the intricate dance of color and light.

Brooks rubbed a hand over the nape of his neck, nonplussed, then moved across the room, ignoring an old member's spiel on how the U.S. should find its own way and shrug off the rest of the world.

Isolationists annoyed him. He hadn't spent a decade serving Uncle Sam without firmly believing in what he'd done and what he was doing. And what he was doing right now, well...

A sensible man would back off instantly. Brooks knew who he was, what he'd done. Better than anyone he understood the choices, his choices, that pushed him into an alcoholic stupor twelve years ago. For years he'd pointed the finger of blame at his brother and Amy before realizing the fault lay with him, at least in part.

If he'd been a better fiancé, Amy would have had no reason to stray. A woman couldn't go on indefinitely loving a man who was never home, unavailable to offer comfort and love. He'd been young and foolish not to realize that then.

If he'd chosen to forgive according to God's word, he'd have a family now, a beautiful family, his parents, his brother, Amy, their children. Two nephews and a niece he'd never seen or met, shut off as a result of his temper, his ignorance and an unforgiving spirit. God help him, his anger had almost resulted in someone's death, at his hands.

Unforgivable behavior.

Theirs or his?

Both, he decided as he nodded and smiled his way across the room. Or at least it seemed so at the time. Now?

Right now all he could see was Rita, the smile she offered one of the older gals in AA, the laugh she shared with Kim, her look commiserate. Kim's job had just been downsized and the stress of looking for work showed in her eyes, her furrowed brow. She was her mother's caretaker, a job Kim took seriously, and bills needed to be paid. It was good to see her laugh with Rita, talk with her, a pair of new friends brought together by a common addiction. Strange and wonderful, all at once.

He couldn't help but compare this Rita with the woman who'd come in over a year ago, ashen, embarrassed, her hair dulled by lack of care and nutrients. Whiskey wasn't exactly a multivitamin. When a drunk trades healthy calories for liquor, the body suffered from lack of nourishment.

He'd been pushed to her side that night, a niggle of the Holy Spirit for certain, a hand to his back, guiding him to her side. Smiling at her. Encouraging her.

Kim was her sponsor, Rita's go-to person in a crisis, but Brooks played his backup role well. He could advise, mentor, tweak and tease, all in the name of friendship. Although for the life of him he'd never had a friend draw him this way, calling to him like a lighthouse beckons a ship to safe harbor.

But a man who cold-shouldered his parents for loving both sons, a man with a heart hardened by his own hand, didn't play at games of romance. Brooks didn't deserve a fairy-tale ending. Why then, around Rita, did it seem possible? Even plausible?

She turned and spotted him, delight at his presence brightening her eyes, her cheeks.

Her sparkle inspired his grin as he approached, his heart lighter. Of course, so was his bank account after his morning expedition in Canton, but the thought of telling her he'd bought the store made him almost giddy inside.

"Hey." He reached her side and handed her a cup of tea.

"Thank you." She smiled up at him and nodded to the room at large. "A good crowd tonight."

Brooks nodded. "I'm never sure if that's good or bad. It's good that people are seeking the strength in numbers, but is it indicative of harder times that so many come?"

"And here I was just enjoying that people wanted time together, fellowship, bonded in grace and determination to do well. Do we have to analyze everything, Brooks? Can't some things just be?"

When she was right, she was right. "I do tend to over-analyze."

"You think?"

"A soldier that fails to read and assess a situation with pin-point accuracy can wind up dead."

"And I didn't even see the battlefield," Rita murmured, teasing. "Silly me." She raised her cup of tea. "My tea is perfect. Thank you for bringing it to me. I saw the crowd at the coffee table and figured I'd wait."

"Whereas I was brave enough to muscle my way in, secure the tea and transport it across the room."

"My hero."

The combination of her look and words melted another little chunk inside him.

He'd been labeled a hero before. He had the medals and certificates to prove it, but it meant little. He may have been pressed into Uncle Sam's service by demand, but once there, he'd been unafraid to prove his worth. Not for awards and commendations. For peace. Equity. Justice for the weary, the oppressed, the downtrodden.

Those heroics lay behind him. A different sort stood before him, the chance to be a hero for Rita's sake. He knew she needed friends. Scores of people had turned against her when Tom's scheming left them without funds. Some forgave, understanding their own responsibility in the mess. If something sounds too good to be true, it usually is.

Others...not so much.

Rita sipped her tea again, the soft curve of her cheek tipped in a smile as Kim leaned in, whispered. Rita rolled her eyes, glanced up at Brooks then nodded, her move conspiratorial.

Brooks edged in. "It's rude to talk about other people when they're standing right there."

Her smile deepened. She turned, that soft lock of hair that refused to be tamed slipping to hide her face, her cheek. He raised a gentle hand and tucked the errant strand back, the feel of her cheek, her ear, her hair a winsome tug on his heart.

And on his soul.

"Kim was just saying you look particularly wonderful tonight," Rita whispered, her eyes sparking humor at his expense. "She wondered if there was a girl involved."

"Did you tell her there might be?" Brooks watched as she studied his face, his eyes, hearing his words, reading his intent.

She blushed delectably.

He leaned in once more. "Tell Kim yes. There is a girl. And if she needs more details to catch me later. We've got a meeting to start."

In silent salute, he touched his forehead to hers, nodded to Kim and headed to the front of the room, leaving Rita speechless. For the moment, at least. With women, lack of speech rarely lasted long.

But every now and again it paid off to play the element of surprise. From the expression he read on Rita's face when he turned from the old wooden pulpit that now served as a speaker's podium, surprise won, hands down.

Score one for the former army captain.

One coffee into fellowship time, Brooks rose, clutching Rita's prospectus in one hand and his coffee mug in the other. "Guys, Rita and I need to discuss some business she's got going so we're going to duck into a booth by the windows for a while. Good seeing you all tonight."

A few eyebrows shifted up and a couple of knowing smiles marked their exit, but Rita ignored them.

Mostly.

Brooks was a great friend and a powerful mentor, but strong, silent types that hug the community sideline weren't all that attractive.

Yeah, right.

And his take-charge attitude could grate on a girl's nerves. Hadn't Rita worked hard to become more positive, more assertive, less wishy-washy? Why would she even consider going from the frying pan into the fire?

Brooks is nothing like Tom. Nothing. That's like comparing fire and rain, oil and water. Doesn't mix, no way, no how, end of story.

And he shied away from church even though she knew his beliefs, understood his strong faith, had listened to him expound on gifts of the Spirit countless times at meetings. Having the grace and moxie to attend services, pray with others, well...

That's what people did. Normal people. More than anything else, Rita longed to be considered normal. She'd had enough above and below average to last a lifetime.

Nope. Normal was the goal. Who would have thought it would be all that difficult to reach?

She sighed, eyed Brooks, then couldn't hid her surprise when he slid into the booth alongside her instead of across from her, his proximity jacking her heart rate up and her hastily erected walls down.

He smiled and held the prospectus up as his hip bumped hers. "It's easier if we can both see what I'm talking about." He pointed to the other side of the booth. "I don't read well upside down."

A part of her bought his reasoning. Another part saw and read the twinkle in his gray eyes and couldn't help but smile. "By all means, Brooks. Your comfort is my first concern."

"Is it now?" The twinkle eased into a grin.

Rita jabbed him with her right elbow. "No, I'm kidding. Precious little prods you out of your comfort zone."

"Making your job that much easier."

He opened the folder as she gave him a look of exaggerated disbelief, eyes wide, brow thrust up. "Your opening is great, the brief overview, the quick synopsis of plan, then the prospectus itself. Your weak part is here, in procuring the right site, facts and figures."

"How so?" She leaned in, the warm, woodsy scent of him washing over her. For just a moment she wondered what it would be like to nestle her cheek against the soft cotton of his shirt at day's end, to snuggle into shoulders that broad and brawny, the feel of his late-day whiskers against her skin.

Then she shook herself out of fantasyland, reiterating to herself every reason why she should remain uninvolved with anyone. Three good reasons were at home right now. Liv needed her mother's example and guidance into adulthood. Brett needed someone to believe in his prowess, his efforts both on and off the soccer field. And Skeeter...

Figuring out Skeeter would take time, effort and moxie on Rita's part. And maybe a little jail time.

Reason enough right there to fight off this attraction to Brooks. He couldn't stand the kid, and since Rita and the kid were a package, that about clinched things.

But the guy smelled totally, absolutely wonderful, a hint of spice mixing with the scent of sawn wood and North Country fresh air.

"Are you with me, Reet?"

He was spewing something about location, location, location. Hadn't Steve Laraby touted the same thing when she'd gone over the ideal site in Canton with a fine-tooth comb?

Ideal but out of her price range.

"You're coming in loud and clear," she assured him. "But I've been through the facts and figures on the Main Street, Canton, site and I can't afford the rent Horace wants with the necessary upgrades, even with full financing."

"I saw that," Brooks explained, nodding. "So I bought

the building today. Figured my rent would be about half of Horace's."

"You what?"

He grinned, easing back in his seat. "Bought the building."

"No."

"Yes."

"You couldn't have."

"Could and did."

"Brooks." Rita paused, her head spinning as she tried to wrap herself around this new bit of news. "Why would you do that?"

"Two reasons."

She nodded, frowning.

"First, it's a good investment. Horace understands that but he's beyond the age and stage where he wants to get down and dirty with refurbishing and repairs to build sweat equity. I'm not. I love that kind of thing."

"Okay." Rita drew the word out slowly, partially buying into his reasoning.

"Second, I believe in what you want to do. I'm a businessman, Reet, first and foremost. I love working with wood, but I don't do it for aesthetic value alone. I like making money, running my own place, being in charge."

"Such a guy."

He pressed in a little. "Being a guy who takes charge when necessary isn't a bad thing."

Odd. Coming from him it didn't feel like a bad thing. Tom had been a whole different story.

"As a businessman, I'd be foolish to see a good opportunity for real-estate investment escape me, especially with a possible renter handed to me on a silver platter. I see a win-win situation here."

"How so?"

"I add to my real-estate portfolio, which is never a bad thing if you pay attention to the buy low, sell high mantra. I have a willing renter who's determined to make a go of her business in an area where her business will not only fit but is desperately needed."

"You really think that?"

"I know that. And third, I get to be your landlord."

"To further boss me around."

Brooks dipped his chin in assent, laughter accentuating the tiny crow's-feet of his eyes and the little crease in his forehead. "Bossing you around is fun. Why do you think that is, Reet?"

"Because you grew accustomed to it in the army and old habits die hard?"

"Possibly," he rejoined, disgustingly cheerful. "Or because it's just that much fun to watch you get annoyed."

"You take pleasure in annoying me?"

"For your own good."

"Right." She put her head in her hands, thinking, then angled him a look from between her fingers. "What kind of rent are we talking, Brooks?"

The figure he named drew her upright in her seat. "That's less than half what Horace wanted."

"We'll renegotiate in twenty-four months," Brooks told her. "That way you have two solid years to get your feet on the ground, build a repeat clientele and a commercial side if you want to see about supplying Canton Tech and/or St. Lawrence University with product. Or the local schools. Catering. Weddings, et cetera."

"Brooks, this could make things possible, if I can obtain the loan for start-up costs."

"You brought the list of banks and financial institutions with you?"

She nodded and withdrew the list from her pocket. "Right here."

"Good." All business now, he uncapped a pen from his shirt pocket, adjusted his reading glasses and leaned forward. "Let's pick five to start with, okay? The five most likely. Then we'll move from there if they reject the application."

"You think they will."

He shrugged. "I think these are tough times so we may have

to run a few extra laps around the application process, but I know a good plan when I see one. One of these loan officers will recognize the strong business opportunity this offers and grant the loan. The question is, which one?"

"Didn't bring my crystal ball tonight. Sorry."

He smiled, unconcerned. "We don't need anything other than tenacity to fill out the paperwork, answer the questions and talk the talk. Sell the idea."

That Rita could do. When it came to baking, display and marketing, she could talk circles around most anyone. "Can do."

"That's just the attitude you need to show them," Brooks approved. "Meet their gaze and handle them like you handle me."

"I don't handle you, Brooks."

"You do, you just don't realize it yet. Heaven help both of us when you do."

Rita tried to read meaning behind the words but fell short.

Did he mean she manipulated him, his help, his cooperation, when needed?

She grimaced inside. She wasn't above doing that when necessary. Was that a bad thing? Not when they were friends, right? Wasn't she more than willing to do the same for him?

Of course.

Or did he mean... Absolutely not.

Totally, indisputably impossible. Beyond the realm of possibilities, even.

And yet...

Rita tried to halt the direction her thoughts had taken, that maybe, just maybe, Brooks was talking about something more than business. Than friendship.

Except she wasn't free to allow those meanderings. Neither was he, not really. Somehow or other Brooks was tied to a past he refused to discuss or acknowledge, holed up in his Fort Bragg-style apartment, unfettered to say the least.

And that was being generous.

Rita could count a gazillion reasons why an attraction to

Brooks was a terrible idea for both of them, starting with the fact that they were both drunks.

Former drunks.

Who've both been very successful in recovery.

Rita reached a hand to the one-year chip in her pocket, the smooth metal a familiar calm to her spirit, her thoughts jumbled around business, bakeries and Brooks.

He looked confident and calm, cool and collected, while she felt like her safe, mundane day-to-day world had just tumbled out of orbit.

Could she do this?

Yes. She believed that, heart and soul.

Should she do this?

That was the question of the hour. But didn't she encourage her kids to take hold, take charge, move forward?

Yes, but she had the awesome responsibility of them on her shoulders. Risking their shaky financial security wasn't something to take lightly. If only she could access Tom's pension fund, the one he'd tied to Ed's pension plan, but there'd been no court ruling on that as yet and she understood the very real possibility of the judge ruling in Ed's favor.

No, she had to look at this from a solid vantage point of what *was,* not what could be.

Brooks was behind her, enough so that he bought the building she needed to rent. What a friend.

He pushed forward again, leaning into her just a little. "Don't overthink this. I've made a sound business move and it opens a window of opportunity for you. That's it in a nutshell. If necessary, that's all it ever needs to be."

She turned to him, saw the promise in his eyes, his gaze, his heart.

A promise that said he might be willing to offer more at some point in time, but he didn't want her fretting about that. Not now. Today was about a business agreement between two friends, a contract made to benefit both. *That* she could live with. She reached out a hand and shook his firmly. "A pleasure doing business with you, Brooks."

He grinned, gave her hand a light squeeze and took a long sip of his cooled coffee. "Pleasure's all mine, ma'am."

Chapter Nine

Brooks swung by Rita's house the next evening. Her eyes widened in surprise. She glanced around, then drew her gaze back to him. "Were we supposed to get together for something tonight? Did I forget?"

"Didn't come to see you, ma'am." He nodded behind her, his eyes bright, his expression pointed. "Brett and I have some work to do."

Rita turned, a tiny frown of confusion marking her features. Brett stepped by her, planted a kiss on her cheek and headed down the front steps to Brooks' truck. "See you later, Mom. I'm helping Brooks fix up the bakery. We're buying stuff tonight. I won't be late."

"Is your homework finished?"

"Did it early so we could get this shopping done."

"Shopping?" The look she sent Brooks combined surprise and suspicion. "Who is that boy and what have done with my son, Brooks Harriman? Brett doesn't shop, not ever, at least not without more than his fair share of moaning and groaning."

Brooks sent her an affable grin. "He does if you take him to the right stores. We're picking out lumber. Nails. Wall-board. Backer board. Man stuff. Brett's my new handyman apprentice."

A smile stole across her face, brightening her eyes, lightening her features, making him wish he could inspire it more often.

Then Skeeter screamed something in a shrill voice from upstairs and he couldn't help but cringe.

"Take her, too."

"Um...no."

"You're sure?" Rita sent him a look half teasing, half imploring. "I could sweeten the deal with dessert later."

He laughed. "I'd love the dessert, but not at the expense of that." He sent a pointed look toward the stairs. "This is where motherhood becomes sainted territory."

"Or jail-worthy." Rita nodded toward the front seat of the truck where Brett waited. "Thanks for including him. And for the positive attitude."

He grinned, ignoring the tirade emitting from upstairs. "I have no doubts and can't see wasting time waiting when I've got free time now. That might not be the case in a couple of weeks."

She nodded at his sensibility. "I appreciate it, Brooks."

He didn't say that he'd make time to help her regardless. Let her think it was circumstance that pushed him to grab Brett and start gathering supplies to make Horace's former store a new bakery enterprise.

Brett was a good kid. Strong. Solid. Quieter than Liv and Skeeter. He had a lot of Rita's personality. Favored her in looks, too, except for his brown hair.

He'd become adept at working his aunt Sarah's farm and helped her husband, Craig, with finishing work on Craig's house the year before when he, Liv and Skeeter lived with Sarah in her old bungalow in nearby Pierrepont. The boy was quiet and capable, a great combination. Brooks climbed into the truck, started it and thrust it into gear. He noted Brett's appreciative glance to the hood and nodded. "Five-point-four liter, three-valve Triton V-8, great torque, rough on gas, perfect power in snow and hauls off-road when necessary."

"You like to off-road?"

"Love it. Camp. Trails. Fish."

"Hunting?"

Brooks shook his head. Something about being a soldier

made the idea of tracking things with a gun less appealing than they might have been. Memory spikes? In any case... "No, I don't hunt. Do you?"

"No. I like fishing, though. A lot. Not much time, though."

"Maybe this summer." Brooks negotiated the turn toward the lumber store, then shrugged. "It's hard during the school year with homework and sports and helping your aunt Sarah."

"Exactly."

"And you and Craig did well in last year's tournament." Craig and Brett had placed in the late-summer fishing derby, offering the pair some cold, hard cash, fishing equipment and well-earned respect, a sweet deal for Brett since Craig's family was one of those swindled by Brett's father.

Good family, good people. A tiny stab of regret struck Brooks full in the chest. The Macklins were a strong example of quiet Christianity at work, of a family that hung together in good times and bad. Brooks could take a lesson from Craig and Cade, their parents, their grandmother.

Forgive and forget. For years he'd fought forgiving his family, clinging to old hurts, aged wrongs.

Now, he wondered more if they could forgive *him,* his stubborn pride, his bullheadedness, qualities that made him a top-notch Delta operator but a poor excuse for a son and brother.

Brett's smile interrupted his musings. "The fishing derby was sweet."

"Yes, it was. Once the weather warms a bit, maybe the three of us can go fishing. Leave the women to their own devices."

"I'd like that," Brett admitted. "Liv's not around so much anymore, she's always busy, but Skeeter's a brat and I'd rather be anyplace than with her."

Ouch. While Brooks understood Brett's stand, he knew that left Rita totally holding the bag with Skeeter. Then again, she was the kid's mother, making it her job. Why couldn't the kid just be nice? Normal? Like Brett and Liv.

"She's a handful, that's for sure."

"That's a nice way of putting it." Brett made a face and shook his head. "I don't even have my friends over when she's going to be there because she just goes out of her way to make me mad. Mess things up."

"Why do you think she does that?"

"Don't know and don't care," Brett replied. "I just wish she'd stop."

Brooks couldn't disagree. Hadn't he felt the exact same way around Rita's youngest? And hadn't he done the very same thing, shy away, walk away, leaving Rita to handle it?

Maybe that was part of the problem. Everyone else had the choice to shrug off the kid's behavior and move on.

Rita had no such option.

Would Skeeter try harder to behave if someone else was in charge? Maybe. Maybe not. Her behavior at school was better than at home. That was indicative of something, right? If she could control the behavior at school, that meant she was choosing to lose control at home.

But why? Brooks had no idea.

They pulled into the lumberyard along the contractor's exit, a chill wind browbeating the southwest corner of the building. "I'll be glad when things warm up." Brett tugged his hooded sweatshirt closer as they headed for the door.

"Me, too."

"Where to first?"

Brooks jerked his head left. "Lumber."

"That gets pretty expensive, doesn't it?"

Brooks nodded. "Very. That's why I figured if we do the bulk of the work for your mom, we can save her a bunch of money and that makes the bakery closer to reality."

"She'll love having her own place."

"Yes."

"Before my dad died..."

Brooks' attention jerked up. Brett never talked about his father. Ever. "Yes?"

"Mom had the kitchen set up for business. Not a big business, but people came from all over to buy her cakes, her cookies, her wedding cakes and pies. All that stuff. She loved doing it."

"It made her happy."

"Yeah." Brett paused, quiet, eyeing the lumber area before spotting the first shelf they needed to visit. "I want her happy again."

"She's better, Brett." Brooks kept his voice easy, not wanting to thwart the moment but unwilling to push for too much, too soon. "Much better."

"I know. It's just…" Brett fingered a two-by-four, withdrew it, eyed the slight curve to the far end and set it aside. "We worry a little."

Brooks nodded. "Everybody worries when you're dealing with an alcoholic. You worry about what might mess things up, push them over the edge, make 'em grab that first drink. The one that leads to another, then another…"

"Exactly."

"Life doesn't come with guarantees, though."

Brett shrugged. "I guess not."

"But the one thing I can tell you is that your mom is doing great. I've been in recovery and AA a long time."

Brett slanted his gaze up to Brooks. "I can't see you drunk."

"Good thing. It wasn't pretty. I'm tough and opinionated sober."

Brett smiled, not disagreeing.

"Drunk? I was a total jerk. I'm still ashamed of it now."

"Some things are like that."

Brooks wondered what a kid Brett's age could have on his conscience that made him that empathetic, then realized in this day and age, anything goes. He nodded. "Yes, they are. But I'm proud of your mother. Her work ethic, how hard she's tried to set things right, how much she does. What that woman fits into a day boggles the mind."

"That's why you're helping her? Helping us?"

Brett's expression challenged him, looking for honesty. Brooks couldn't ignore the look. Wouldn't ignore the look. "I like her, Brett. A lot."

"What happens if you stop liking her? What happens to her then?"

Smart kid, wondering if Rita might tumble off the wagon of sobriety if they had a falling-out, if their friendship hit the wall. "Who can say? But I've discovered if you let fear prevent you from taking chances, life looms pretty long and dull."

"Dull beats insane."

Brooks agreed as he withdrew more two-by-fours for Brett's critical eye. "But it doesn't trump happiness. And you and your mom and your sisters deserve some happiness in your lives."

"Can't argue that."

"Me, either."

"What do you make of this one?" Brett held up a board. "These knots would make nailing a pain, wouldn't they?"

"Yup. Whereas this one—" Brooks held one up where the natural knot in the wood lay more centered "—is one we can work around. The knot's in tight enough that we can nail from both sides and be fine."

"What are we building with these?"

"A new wall." Brooks set another two-by-four on the pile and counted. "We need eight more. I'll show you the bakery site later this week, when you don't have soccer practice."

"Friday?"

Brooks shook his head. "I've got a meeting on Friday. Several new people on hand."

"They look up to you."

Brooks brushed that off. "They look up to anyone who's been sober awhile. The beginning is always toughest."

"Like when a plane takes off."

"Great analogy."

"Mom used it when she explained that getting off the booze was hardest in the beginning and in times of crisis. That's kind of why Liv and I avoid problems. Making them. Telling her about them."

"She wouldn't want to be shut out," Brooks told him, "but I know she appreciates how you two work to keep the peace. That's not always easy, especially at your age."

"My age?"

Brooks gave him a frank look. "You're growing up.

Physically, mentally and emotionally. That's a lot of powerful stuff going on."

"Is this conversation heading toward weird? Because I'm okay if it doesn't."

Brooks laughed out loud. "No weird, I promise. But if you ever need to talk things out—need a guy—Craig and I are available. With your dad gone there might be times you feel alone. But you're not."

Chin down, Brett mulled that a moment and shrugged. "You didn't know my dad, Brooks. I was alone when he was around. I think I was the only one in the family not surprised by what happened."

Another rare moment of Brett opening up. Brooks angled his head, patient. "Astute or aware?"

"Aware." Brett stared off into space a few seconds then dragged his gaze back to Brooks. "I overheard him on his cell phone a few times. He didn't think I was all that bright and he'd say things in front of me. I was a kid, but I was old enough to understand what he was saying. Tanking stocks, shelving funds, taking hits, blown equity."

"He said that stuff in front of you?"

"When you're invisible, people don't notice you."

Right about then, Brooks had the urge to do a little serious one-on-one with Tom Slocum, give him a taste of that Brooks of old, the hands-on tough commander.

But Tom was in God's hands now. Brooks could only hope the punishment was tough enough to give Tom Slocum a taste of how he wronged his family, his community, his friends, his children.

"Well, kid, you're pretty visible now, and if we spend the whole night talking like a couple of girls, we'll get nothing done."

Brett laughed. "Don't let Mom hear you talk like that. You'll get an earful."

"Like that doesn't happen on a regular basis." Brooks grinned. "What's next on our list?"

"Plywood and wallboard."

"Next aisle."

"Can do."

"That was nice of you, taking Brett along." Rita started to cut a slice of cake for Brooks, the promised dessert, a nice, normal way to end an evening.

His big hand covered hers, sending sweet warmth up her arm, through her neck, pooling someplace in her gut. For just a moment she rested her cheek against his sleeve, the warm wash of cotton, Tide and lumber soothing.

She felt Brooks grin against her cheek as he repositioned the hand three degrees to the right. "Much better."

She laughed as he stepped back. "Hungry?"

"Starving. Picking out building supplies is tough work."

"Was Brett helpful?"

"The kid's amazing."

Rita preened.

"You've done a great job with him."

"Except for the two years I wasted on whiskey and wallowing, yes. I agree."

Brooks shook his head, his expression easy. "Everything doesn't have to come back around to that, Reet. We all make mistakes, we all flounder, and depression can take us down that road real quick. Hard to put the brakes on."

"I don't like to make excuses for my behavior." She cut the slice of cake, then cut a narrower one for herself. "For me it's better to see it for what it was, deal with my mistakes openly and move on."

"Moving on being key."

"Yes."

"And you have." He stepped forward and turned her to face him. "You're doing great. I'm proud of you."

A little smile edged her lips but the concern in her eyes didn't fade.

"What's up?"

She shook her head. "Skeeter. The bank loans. Me."

His angled head and furrowed brow invited her to continue.

"I keep trying to figure out how I'm going to handle Skeeter and her behavior, my job, the loan applications, Brett and Liv's schedules... With Liv only fifteen, I don't have anyone to help drive them places. It seems like every time I get a half hour to work on something, I have to stop and run here, there or somewhere else. Then I examine my time management at night and it looks good on paper, you know? An hour here, forty minutes there. But it disappears and I'm feeling frustrated that I can't move forward farther, faster."

"Pray for patience."

"Ha."

He gave her an expectant look, very sure, very wise, very Brooks, smug enough to almost get him smacked. "It's tough handing over the reins, giving God total control. Trusting in that timing, that pace."

"But God didn't put me here to lollygag around, spin my wheels and make do. Now that I've finally got a plan, got a chance, I want to take it. Run with it."

He laughed. "Understandable. But since we've got a bunch of work to do on that building, take a breath. Say a prayer. Fill out the applications online first, they're the easiest. Get them in and out of the way. If you need help with them, I'm available."

"I'd be embarrassed to have you see what I owe," Rita admitted, chagrined. "After the fiasco with Tom and my years of drinking, I'm lucky to have a roof over my head. That's half my problem," she admitted. "I'm embarrassed to have those loan officers see what my life looks like in black-and-white. And red."

"They'll notice that, sure. But that's in the past, you avoided bankruptcy through all that mess, you've got a great business head and plan and the power to implement it. Give them credit for seeing between the lines, making a full assessment. Some will turn us down. Some won't. We just don't give up until we find the one willing to take that chance."

"We?"

"I'm your landlord, remember?" Sparks of ivory lightened his gray eyes, crinkled in amusement.

"You won't let me forget."

"Ever."

She laughed and poked him in the chest. "That means when the heat's off or the electric blows a circuit breaker, I call you."

"Please do."

Her heart chugged to a stop, watching him, hearing those words, feeling their depth, their meaning. He studied her, expression warm, caring, a hint of humor softening the craggy planes of a chiseled face.

She moved a half step forward without meaning to. "I will."

The kiss was unexpected, and totally wonderful, the gentle press of Brooks' mouth on hers, the solidity of him, his breadth, his warmth, the sheer strength of him swirling around her, engulfing her in what-ifs.

Sweet. So sweet.

When he paused the kiss she stayed right there, not moving, eyes closed, smiling just a little, knowing she couldn't and shouldn't do this, but old enough and experienced enough to know she thoroughly enjoyed that kiss.

And the kisser.

And when he kissed her again, she liked that one just as much.

"Cake?"

She stepped back, sent him a bemused look, handed him the cake and plunked herself down at the table. "Did you plan that move?"

He sat across from her with his plate but his eyes weren't on the cake. Warm and amused and maybe even the tiniest bit dazed, he kept his gaze on her as if the surprise and wonder of that kiss affected him the same way. Was that possible?

His answer interrupted her analysis. "No. But I've thought about it a long while, and the opportunity afforded itself. Me, you, proximity. A guy's gotta take a chance now and again."

"Except I can't afford chances." Rita met him eye-to-eye. "I can't afford mistakes, things that might push me out of control. I've got three kids to raise and I'm having a heck of a time doing it."

"I try to avoid mistakes myself." The look he sent her curled her toes, made her read between the lines. "But I agree. You and I have a business relationship."

"Yes."

"A partnership of sorts."

"Absolutely."

"And we shouldn't be messing that up with some crazy wild notion of romantic nonsense and happily-ever-afters."

"Exactly. We've been there, done that. Then ended up drunk and disorderly."

He tilted his head, not smiling, not frowning, very staid, total Brooks. "Though if the occasion warrants, I can't in good conscience guarantee a no-kiss policy."

"You're suggesting allowance for friendly pecks on the cheek?"

"I'm suggesting we work together and see what happens."

She sent him her best direct "ain't gonna happen in this lifetime, no way, no how" look. "Nothing's going to happen." Saying the words she had to physically disengage her reaction to his kiss, his teasing, his warmth. "We can't afford mistakes, Brooks. Especially since you'll be in business with me, as my landlord. We can't mess this up. It means too much, there's far too much at stake."

"But we might be able to afford the occasional chance," he argued. He waved his fork toward the plate. "And this cake is marvelous by the way. That lemon filling? Perfect."

"I'm leaving my risk taking to loans, bakeries and business," she told him. "Your friendship means everything to me. I've got no intention of jeopardizing that. Not now. Not ever."

His expression showed acceptance. The teasing glint in his eye said she'd just been targeted as a challenge. If there was one thing she was sure of in this crazy, mixed-up world, it was that Brooks Harriman loved a challenge.

Chapter Ten

The message light on Brooks' answering machine flashed as he stepped into his apartment. He picked up the phone, and pressed the keypad to engage the message. Greg Callahan's voice asked him to call when he got in, regardless of the hour.

Trouble.

He punched in Greg's number, mind spinning, creating worst-case scenarios in the short seconds it took for Greg's phone to ring. Had he waited too long? Had one of his parents…?

He refused to think that. When Greg finally picked up, Brooks feigned a calm demeanor. "What's up?"

Greg wasted no words. "Your brother's got colorectal cancer. His treatment's been unsuccessful."

Brooks wondered at the way his heart lurched. He bit back a sigh and shook his head, two fingers pinched at the bridge of his nose. "Prognosis?"

"Not long, Captain." Greg always reverted to Brooks' title when making a point. He hadn't used it in a long time. "You're running out of time."

"*I'm* not." His emphasis on the pronoun weighed his point.

"You're a fool if you don't set this right while you have the chance," Callahan retorted. "Make your peace. This will be hard enough on your parents without feeling like they failed you, too."

"Coming back, bringing everything back to mind, dragging

it all up? If Paul's that sick, I don't see how that could be good for anyone. Least of all Paul and Amy."

"Cowardly response."

"I'd say levelheaded. We're talking a lot of years, Callahan."

"When I told you it would help your mission to sobriety if you moved away from the area, I didn't mean for you to disappear into North Country obscurity forever. Do you have to do everything to the extreme?"

He did, Brooks realized. When he put his hand to something, he went a little OCD in his quest to do it right, make it better, stronger, faster, longer. This time he did sigh. "I guess I do."

"Then recognize that and realize you need to deal with this now. I've been a recovered drunk a long time, Captain. I know how things eat at a man, gnawing until he caves under pressure over stuff that shouldn't matter. Take care of this now, while you have the chance."

Go back. See his family. Make amends. Ask forgiveness.

Brooks stared at the blank wall in front of him. Was Greg right? Would this chew on him, relentless and unsolvable after Paul's death, knowing he could have stepped forward and didn't?

And what did he fear most? Their rejection or their forgiveness?

Hard to know.

Or was it fear that seeing Amy and Paul happy might push buttons he'd left buried a long time ago? Push him over the top.

He hadn't been tempted by the bottle in years, and that level of confident sobriety was sought after by a reformed drunk. He'd achieved it, but he'd be lying to say facing the past didn't unnerve him.

Greg was right. Cowardly fear held him back, but he'd been down the road of a drunk before. He understood it like no other, had almost killed a man in a stupid, drunken brawl until Greg showed up in uniform, broke things up and hauled him to the slammer.

He owed Greg so much. If it hadn't been for Sergeant Greg Callahan, Brooks might have been sitting in jail these past twelve years, not building a business and a solid reputation in Grasse Bend, New York.

Still...

"I can't make this decision right now. I need to think things through. Weigh them up."

"Got your Bible handy?"

"Always."

"Try Luke, chapter six. Or Matthew, chapter seven. Maybe it's time you started looking at things anew."

Brooks was familiar with both passages, had used them often in his righteous indignation that the fornicating minister won the girl while the ardent soldier suffered pain and peril. Both Luke and Matthew noted this part of the Sermon on the Mount, the lesson taught with strength and maybe a touch of humor: "How can you say to your brother, 'Brother, let me take the speck out of your eye,' when you yourself fail to see the plank in your own eye? You hypocrite, first take the plank out of your eye, and then you will see clearly to remove the speck from your brother's eye." Once he'd finished college and joined the army, he realized he was meant to take on challenges.

Brooks feared little in his forty-two years, born to adventure, like a duck to water. Hadn't he spent his boyhood doing that very thing while Paul hung back, older but weaker, always cautious and questioning, pondering what to do, indecisive and unsure?

Brooks always knew what to do. Part of good soldiering lay in the think-on-your-feet mentality God had gifted him. He did better with quick decision making, taking tough stands, following through. If the past decade-plus was any indication, Brooks didn't do quite so well with putting things on hold.

His family situation had festered, growing out of control. Why had he never called? Never contacted his parents, his dad, his mother? Thoughts of Carol Anne Harriman's face wrenched his spirit, her soft hands, the quick and ready smile, the laughter he'd grown up with. She'd loved his humor, his brash boldness, his bravado.

He missed her so much, but he'd been gone a long time. He'd hurt her, hurt his dad, hurt all of them. The Mother's Days, Father's Days, birthdays, Christmases. All gone, lost, ignored, never to be retrieved. Time wasted while he built a life alone.

But going home, apologizing, dredging up the past that dogged his heels, sent a quiver of fear down his spine.

"I'll pray on it, Greg. Best I can do right now."

"Pray fast."

The intractable click of Greg's phone hit Brooks dead center.

Which was exactly why Greg did it, he was sure.

Brooks eyed the Bible on the coffee table. Someone had once told him the Bible wasn't coffee-table reading. They were so wrong. He liked it there, ever present, dependable when men were not.

But he walked past the bound volume, refusing its wisdom. He was in no mood to read about Job's long-suffering patience. "Welcome to my world," he muttered, heading to his room. In boot-camp fashion everything was put away just so, folded or hung if not tossed in the laundry hamper. Life on a cot had taught him to do it now and do it right. Not a bad credo to live by.

He pushed aside twinges of conscience brought on by Greg's words. Soldiers developed a sleep-on-demand skill that he hadn't needed in a very long time.

He used it tonight.

Right until the clanking clatter of his garbage can dragged him from his bed in the wee small hours. Scowling, he pulled on a sweatshirt as the noise continued, the rattle and roll of tin a dead giveaway. At least it wasn't so cold tonight, a hint of spring softening the blow of his predawn nemesis. He'd rolled the cans out front in anticipation of the early morning garbage truck, hoping the past few nights of no access had thwarted the dog's appetite.

No.

Brooks went out his back door, thinking his clandestine move might surprise the mutt.

Not even close.

A flash of copper fur was his only visual as the dog veered around the front of the building, dodged left and disappeared into the wooded back lot again. Brooks had seen enough to note no collar. He'd heard no jangle of tags, labeling the dog a stray, most likely.

"Come here, pal. Let's see what you've got, one-on-one."

To Brooks' surprise, the dog's muzzle reappeared at the woods' edge as Brooks rounded the corner of the store. Brooks stepped forward, frowning, then squatted. "Come on, pal. Head on over here. Things would work much better between us if you just came begging at the door rather than ransacking my place night after night."

The dog's tail wagged as if offering a flag of peace. His head was cocked to the right, the canine expression quizzical. The soft glow of the dusk-to-dawn parking lights bathed the dog's face while his hindquarters remained shadowed.

Blame impatience, lack of sleep, Callahan's news about Paul.

Brooks edged forward before the dog was ready. Hackles raised, the dog spun about and disappeared at a quick clip, the pale ivory of his tail a feathery wisp in the slanted light.

Brooks surveyed the mess, and once again regathered his strewed garbage. He placed the cans back where they'd been, realizing the dog was obviously smarter than his human opponent. He went inside and opened three cans of chicken noodle soup, poured them into a stainless-steel three-quart kettle, added some rice cereal squares and put the interesting concoction on the porch step.

Logic said he shouldn't feed a stray.

The Bible said otherwise. In any case, a well-fed dog might not scour garbage cans with the same fervor of a half-starved one.

When I was hungry, you fed me....

When I was in prison, you comforted me. Thoughts of Paul's illness sprang to mind, his prognosis bleak.

Hmm. The dog was one thing, an entity Brooks might not savvy but could help control by taking charge, offering food rather than having his garbage burglarized on a regular basis.

Paul?

A part of him longed to comfort his brother in his time of need. Embrace his parents. A bigger part figured he'd blown that chance a long time ago. How cheeky it would be to show up now, the prodigal, shifting much-needed attention from Paul to him.

Try as he might, the late-night hour and lack of sleep didn't allow intelligent analysis. He went back to bed, and tossed and turned until his cell-phone alarm told him it was time to greet the day. Disgruntled, he got out of bed, got dressed, then stepped out onto the porch stoop to retrieve the morning paper.

The empty pot told him his dog friend had returned for a late-night supper or early morning breakfast. The garbage cans stood where Brooks had placed them, untumbled, untouched, the dog's appetite appeased by Brooks' slapdash pot of doggy stew.

The thought of the dog's full stomach soothed Brooks' stress level. Somewhere the dog lay curled in a cozy ball of copper-toned fur, tail tucked, tummy full. Regardless of the ramifications, that scenario made Brooks feel good.

Chapter Eleven

"Brooks." There was no denying the leap of Rita's heart or the quick infusion of warmth when she saw Brooks striding through the grocery-store bakery a little after 7:00 a.m. She sent a quizzical look to the clock on the wall before angling it back to him. "What are you doing here?"

Raising his left hand, he waved colorful slips of slim card-stock. "If you won't come to the paint chips, the paint chips will come to you."

"You brought them?" Relief colored her tone. "I no more than walked in the door this morning and they asked if I could stay late. Between that and the kids' schedules tonight, I figured I'd have to run to the hardware store on my lunch." She hesitated, a little overcome by his thoughtfulness, then flashed him another smile. "Thank you."

"You're welcome. The dog bandit decided I'd had enough sleep around four a.m. and Home Depot opened at six, so..." He shrugged. "Figured we could get one more thing accomplished. And this way, you get to have lunch."

"Yes." She met his smile and read comfort in his eyes. Caring. Compassion. As if he empathized with the chopped-up time frames that ruled her days. "We could..." She hesitated again, wondering if asking him to lunch pushed her over the just-friends line.

Probably.

"Yes?" He angled his head, his expression saying he read her mind and was waiting for her to make a move.

"Um…"

He sighed, rubbed a hand through his hair and arched a questioning brow. "Would you like to have lunch together?"

"Yes."

The speed of her response made him grin, humor replacing the look of question. "You could have just said so."

"I know. But since you did, I don't have to."

He glanced at the clock behind her. "What time are you free?"

"Twelve-thirty."

He jerked his head toward the small café in the front corner of the sprawling grocery store. "I'll meet you in the coffee shop. We'll grab a sandwich, decide on colors for the front of the bakery, then I can get the paint and continue the remodeling."

"Since you have all this free time right now."

His slight flush let her know he was prioritizing the bakery regardless of other commitments. "Right."

She couldn't help herself. Reaching up she laid her palm against his cheek, grateful for his time, his friendship, his confidence in her. The strength he seemed so willing to share. "You're a good guy."

"Yeah. Well." He shrugged, embarrassed.

She stepped back, the day suddenly seeming not so long and dragged out as it had five minutes before. "Twelve-thirty."

He drew a breath and smiled. "It's a date."

Did he know what those words did to her heart? As he headed toward the front he paused and turned back, then dropped her a grin and a wink, his expression saying more than words ever could.

Oh, yeah. He knew exactly what effect he had on her. And from the look on his face, he was totally enjoying it.

"You've looked better, Toots." Brooks gave his curly-haired sales clerk a concerned look later that morning, thinking she might faint. Or hurl. He edged back, uneasy, not exactly hoping to embrace any more drama after last night's phone call from Callahan and the dog's impromptu backyard trash party.

"I'm okay."

"You sure? You look—" Ghastly? Awful? Dead on her feet?

Brooks faltered. A pretty young thing like Tootsie Lawrence wouldn't appreciate those descriptions. But she'd been unwell for a while. A sudden thought struck him. "Toots, are you avoiding the doctor because you have no health insurance?"

Tootsie inhaled through her nose, exhaled slowly and gave him a wan smile. "I hooked up with that state program."

Her response relieved him. He'd offered her a choice of higher pay or a smaller paycheck coupled with health insurance. She'd opted for the increased paycheck, reasoning she was young and healthy.

But now?

"I'm worried about you," he admitted, refusing to pretend otherwise. "If you need time off, or if there's something wrong, I want you to tell me. You're an important part of North Country Woodcrafters."

She started to cry.

No, it couldn't be. Impossible. Hadn't they just gone through this the week before?

He hated women's tears. They were so…feminine. Awkwardly, he patted her back and grabbed tissues from under the counter. "What can I get you? M&M's? Raisinets? Maybe a couple of Twix bars?"

"I'm all right."

"You're not," he insisted. "And women get weepy over three things," he continued, ticking off on his fingers. "Sappy movies, lack of chocolate and a rush of hormones."

"How about a hat trick? You know, three in one?"

"Nuclear holocaust pales in comparison?"

She dabbed her eyes. Blew her nose.

"You sure you've got enough chocolate?"

This time she laughed. "Yes, Boss, I'm fine. Just a little run-down." Her eyes shifted left, then down, the move betraying her. She was dodging the truth, but why?

He had no idea, but he'd been an elite soldier long enough to recognize the maneuver.

He was also her friend. That meant lines drawn in the sand were respected.

On top of that, she was engaged to a soldier stationed in Iraq. That stirred memories he'd kept buried for years. In some ways it helped, though he'd been blindsided a couple of times with recollections that touched raw nerves. Despite the tweaks, he hadn't considered drinking. Not even a thought. Maybe that was why he felt he could take a chance with Rita. Extend the parameters of his safety net to include her.

And three kids, two of whom he liked.

"You need something, Boss?"

"Just thinking. Do kids grow out of being brats?"

If the question surprised her, she masked the emotion. "If they're young enough. I used to watch the Borden kids outside of Malone. No discipline, no follow-through. A rough bunch."

"Was that where your aunt lived when you were little?"

"Yup. Brushton. Very rustic, rural. She had her little farm plot with lots of animals, fruits and vegetables, a real seventies throwback kind of gal. Driving to Canton and Potsdam seemed big."

Brooks grinned.

"But those Borden kids were terrors. They lived on a gravel road, off the main drag. Their little girl, Dana? Doing time now for armed robbery. The fits that kid threw." Tootsie shook her head, remembering. "Temper tantrums galore. Wouldn't listen to anyone. Of course," she continued, rising to open the store for business, "nobody made her behave. Just said it was a stage she was going through."

A chill coursed down Brooks' spine. Hadn't Rita used those exact words? He raised a brow, wishing he had some experience. "But some kids do go through stages like that, right?"

Tootsie turned the key and shrugged. "Earlier, maybe. Like three or four. By the time a kid's seven or eight, that nonsense should be long gone." She splayed her hands, palms down, making her point.

Brooks couldn't disagree. The fact that Rita's youngest was adept at throwing fits meant she was well practiced. Skeeter's brattiness made corporal punishment seem reasonable.

Infiltrating Iraqi defense lines hadn't fazed him, but an out-of-control seven-year-old drove him crazy.

And yet…she was just a kid. Despite her behavior, Skeeter deserved to be around people who loved her.

Maybe Tootsie was wrong. Dana Borden might have been a glitch. Most little girls grew up to be wonderful members of society, right?

He scolded himself as he worked on a new hutch design. Liv would inlay tiny tiles across the top, fitting polished ceramic diamonds and triangles into a patchwork quilt pattern. Mullioned panes of glass in the upper door, some clear, some stained, reflected the tile tones below. Berry red, forest green, ivory and gold. A hint of blue. Warm tones that said home and family.

The hutch was for Rita. He hadn't set out to design the piece for her, but the longing in her voice when she touched pretty things had clinched the decision.

As long as Skeeter didn't take a hammer to the artful piece. Throw something in a fit of anger.

Brooks eyed the painstaking work, the level of detail he had devoted to this piece, wanting the elegant cupboard beautiful for Rita even as he wrestled urges to push her away.

Smoothing a hand across the wood, he studied it, intent. Under his hand stood a piece of furniture, no more, no less. Certainly not as important as a child's welfare. Even if the child was one of the least likable on the planet. Where was Nanny 911 when you needed her?

"Lord, I'm over a barrel on this," Brooks prayed. "I'm attracted to the mother but can't stand the child. Her selfishness irritates me and Rita's inaction drives me crazy.

"Help me find positive things in Skeeter. Something of redeeming value." He shook his head as he surveyed the pristine dovetailing. "You asked the little children to come to You. You drew the shunned to your side, regardless of age, welcoming them." Brooks was willing to bet that none of those children, Jew or Gentile, held a candle to Aleta Rose Slocum.

"I don't know how to do that. I don't have much experience in these matters."

Admitting that helped. It seemed to pinpoint the crux of the problem. Perhaps if he studied child development, he'd have an easier time with Skeeter.

He'd order books and do what he'd been military trained to do. Study the enemy, then launch a well-constructed attack to their weak side. If Skeeter Slocum actually had a weak side.

Somehow he doubted it.

"Soup?" Brooks eyed Rita's bowl of chowder, then his foot-long hoagie. "That's it?"

"It's not soup, it's chowder," she told him, reaching for her pocket. "Way more filling."

"And pie," Brooks added as he slipped a piece of chocolate cream onto her tray.

"But—"

"And I'm buying, so get your hand out of your pocket. What kind of guy takes a girl on a grocery-store date and makes her pay? You've been hanging with the wrong fellas, Reet. Tea?" He jutted his chin toward the tea service just beyond the register, his head tilted in question.

"Yes, thanks, and I haven't been hanging with any fellows at all," she retorted, partly amused, partly annoyed. "And I can buy my own lunch."

"Next time." He paid the cashier then followed Rita to a corner table. "I'm perfectly willing to be a millennium man and let you take me out on occasion."

"Except we're not going out, remember?"

"Got it." His grin said otherwise and did ridiculous things to her heart, making it impossible to hold her ground. And when he was this close, the last thing she wanted to do was hold her ground. "So." He laid color swatches on the table between them. "Pick."

Rita studied the colors, readjusted the chips a few times, then nodded and tapped a finger. "This, this and this."

"Dark green, red and ivory."

She frowned. "Woodland Copse, Cranberry Chalet and Provincial White."

Brooks drew an *x* on each color. "A rose by any other name..."

"Wouldn't be nearly as pretty," she cut in, then nodded toward the color-tinted slips. "These will give me a base to use different color accents all year. I can brighten them in the summer, warm them in the fall and winter. Perfect."

"You've got a good eye, Reet," Brooks admitted. "Liv got that from you, that appreciation for color and balance. She might not look like you, but she carries a lot of your characteristics, your talents."

"You think so?" Rita smiled, the compliment especially dear since Liv looked so much like her father.

"Absolutely. And she's great with people. She works well on the sales floor and in the clean room. A talented young lady."

"Thank you." It wasn't easy to accept the compliment, knowing she'd messed things up for so long, but AA had taught her to move beyond equating everything with the past. While it was hard to do sometimes, today it seemed easier. Brooks' effect?

Entirely possible. "This pie is amazing."

He noted her empty soup bowl with a teasing look. "I don't think I've ever seen soup disappear quite so quickly. Hungry?"

"Yes. And you were right, the pie is a perfect addition."

"I'm a pretty smart guy."

"So you say." Rita licked her fork, fairly certain that dark chocolate and whipped cream were an award-winning combination. "Are you working on the bakery today?"

"As soon as we're done here. Since I got an unexpectedly early start..."

She laughed.

He grimaced. "I figured I'd head over there and begin the preliminary stuff with a crowbar and a sledgehammer."

"I can help tonight."

Brooks leaned forward, the glint in his eyes sending warmth throughout her. "I might be talked into letting you buy me lunch on occasion and even help put things back together, but the breakdown? The sledgehammer?" He shook his head. "That one I'll do with a couple of buds from AA. You get to help with the gentler stuff."

Rita drew herself upright. "I'm perfectly capable..."

He shushed her with two fingers to her mouth, the pads both tender and rough. "Capability isn't the issue. Safety is. And you have enough to do. Change the things you can, remember? It's okay to ask for help."

She knew that, but skated a thin line between asking for help and being needy. But Brooks was right. She could only do so much, and do it well. His constant help was appreciated. She nodded, the touch of his fingers sending her thoughts spiraling back to last night's kiss.

Kisses.

He winked, saying his thoughts had gone in the same direction.

Lucky for both of them, her lunch break was over. She stood abruptly, breaking the connection. "Gotta get back to work."

He smiled, stood and swept the table a glance. "I'll take care of this. Thanks for going out with me."

"But—" His teasing grin stopped her objection. She paused. Sighed. Then smiled, deciding to pick her battles rather than feed his ego. "It was the best lunch I've had in a long time."

The tender look her words inspired made her heart flutter. He stepped forward, head angled, gentle caring warming his gaze. "I'm glad."

Rita's phone rang as she walked in the door from an extended bakery shift. She read Kim's number on the display and grabbed the receiver before the call went to voice mail. "Kim. Hey. What's up?"

"My mom's sick."

"Oh, Kim." Rita bathed the words in commiseration. Kim's mother had been housebound since suffering a massive stroke the year before. Her improvement had been slow and unsteady, but Kim had tried to manage her care around her job, her AA meetings and regular household tasks, not an easy maneuver. Her recent layoff from work had been a financial blow but it offered time with her ailing mother, a positive aspect of unemployment. "Is it bad?"

"It's always hard to tell," Kim explained. "Because her body doesn't cooperate, she can't do or say the normal things we'd do to explain what's wrong."

"Does she need hospitalization?"

Kim sighed. "That's part of the problem. Some say yes, some say no, and then the insurance gets muddled about who's right."

Rita had no clue what to say. Dealing with insurance was no walk in the park. "Stand your ground with them. Be the squeaky wheel if you need to be."

"I hate that."

"We all do. But sometimes it's just downright necessary. Do you need anything? Food? Help? Need me to spell you so you can get out for a bit?" Rita knew Kim's new free time offered way too many hours of at-home thinking time for her friend.

"Maybe later this week. I just needed to let someone know because I won't be at tonight's meeting."

"I'll fill you in on who's doing what and let you know what Katy Lee wears."

Kim laughed out loud, a good sign. Katy Lee liked to garner attention with outrageous costumes, citing her artistic bent as a professor of fine arts as reason enough to express herself, so her outfits were fair game for discussion. "I'll look forward to it. Thanks, Rita."

"You're welcome. And I'll be praying for your mom. And you."

"We both appreciate it."

Rita hung up the phone and thought hard. Kim's sacrifice

for her mother smacked of love, loud and clear, despite their problems during Kim's bout with alcoholism.

Maybe there was hope for a better relationship with her own mother as time went on. Maybe it wouldn't always be a competition. More than anything, Rita longed for peace in her family. Too many years of drama had already passed. Peace would be good.

She dialed her mother's number but got the answering machine. She left a quick message then hung up, half-ashamed for feeling relieved.

"Who were you talking to?"

Skeeter's voice. The look. The cocked hip. Rita took note of the entire picture and made a quick and probably too-long-delayed decision to regain control of Skeeter's behavior. She only prayed she wasn't too late.

"Your tone of voice needs improvement. Try again."

Skeeter assumed a bored expression, tapped a toe and huffed.

Rita stood and headed for the kitchen counter to start dinner. "Let's do your homework right here in the kitchen. That way I can help if you need it and make supper at the same time."

"I'd rather do it upstairs."

Translation: I'd rather not do it at all and make it a struggle later.

"You can go upstairs and play once it's done." Rita handed her a glass of juice and a sliced apple, then nodded toward the table. "Have a seat. I'll be right here if you need me."

"Great." The word was sarcastic, but a hint of grudging respect brightened Skeeter's gaze as she plunked herself into a chair. With exaggerated movements, she pulled her take-home folder from her backpack, sifted through papers and withdrew a math sheet and a spelling list. Rita quizzed her on the spelling words, then offered advice on the second math problem. Other than that, Skeeter completed the assignments independently and in record time.

Rita noted that with a nod of appreciation. "Twenty minutes of reading and you're done."

Skeeter eyed the clock, surprised and pleased. "And it's not even four-thirty."

"Amazing what happens when you get right to it." Rita sent a pointed look to the table. "By the time you're done you'll have the whole evening to clean your room."

"But Norrie…"

"Will have to wait until that bedroom passes my inspection," Rita finished for her. "I do believe we've had this discussion before."

"But—"

"No buts. Homework. Clean room. Free time. In that order. And since you surprised yourself with how fast the homework went, you might find the same is true of your room."

Skeeter's dark look meant that most likely wouldn't be the case, but Rita refused to cave.

Change the things you can….

Rita intended to do just that.

Chapter Twelve

"Exactly like that, Liv." Brooks smiled as Liv fit a tiny tile into its assigned space on the practice piece, a cutting board he'd designed. He'd kept the allotted space simple and chose two-inch tiles to allow Liv leverage for cutting and positioning. He'd formed the board base with an opening to accommodate either whole tiles in simplistic rows or a more adventurous design.

Now it was up to Liv.

She sat back, head angled, eyes scrunched, studying the hard maple rectangle. Then she won his heart a little more when she smoothed her palm across the wood's surface, face serene, a loving touch of respect for the tree, the grain, the wood. Leaning in, she breathed deep, the scent of freshly sanded maple drawing a smile.

"I love this smell."

Brooks grinned. "Yeah?"

"Oh, yes." She inhaled again, sat back and nodded, pleased. "All of this, actually. I love the feel of the wood, the scent, the texture of the grains, so different from wood to wood."

"Like that hickory over there." Brooks waved a hand to a mellow-toned table, the wild grain of the wood running amok through the sides and doors, then evening a bit across the top.

"If that's hickory, then it's one of my favorites," Liv declared.

"The color or the grain?"

"Both." Liv nodded that way, then brought her eyes back to the maple. "But this has its own place in my heart, too."

"How so?"

She waved a hand across the surface once more, then lifted one shoulder in a slight shrug. "Grandma Barnes has a lot of maple stuff in her house outside of Albany."

"Pretty?"

"Very. And Grandma's the kind that doesn't change anything, ever, so the rooms are exactly as they were when Mom was little."

"Seriously?" Brooks found that hard to imagine, then pictured his boring apartment and counted the years. Okay, not so hard to imagine. "Don't most women change things around regularly? Move this here, that there?"

"Not Grandma. And you'd best not try it, either," Liv laughed, then sighed. "And for as pretty as it all is, everything polished and dusted, and the dust ruffles all crisp and neat, the bedcovers totally unwrinkled...it's not homey."

Ah, things were making a little more sense now, the conversations he'd overheard with Rita's mother.

"It looks cozy, like one of those country magazines that make you feel like you can just step inside, sit down and have a cup of coffee or a glass of tea, but it's not really like that. You wouldn't dare."

"I see."

"So while I like the pretty, smooth finish of the maple, it reminds me that not everything is as it seems, you know? But those tables—" Liv jerked her head left toward the hickory "—they're solid, tough, rugged. You don't feel like they're going to mark or scar if you actually use them."

"I'm glad you like them." Brooks kept it simple, but he'd learned a lot from a few short sentences. Rita had gone from a mother who liked things just so to a husband with the very same requirements. Knowing that gave him a better insight into her more relaxed attitude about the house, housework, clutter and chaos.

Dishevelment equated with normal, and wasn't that what

Rita often said? She was striving for normal? Her perception of normal included a lived-in house, busy kids and a business of her own. Liv's insight gave Brooks a better understanding of why that was.

Interesting. Very interesting.

Liv sat back, eyed the board, the tiles, then him. "Do I have to just plunk these in, all in a row?"

Another chunk of his heart melted. He smiled and eased back. "No. Design it any way you want."

Her eyes lit, the artist within springing free. "Seriously?"

He laughed. "Yes. What did you have in mind?"

"I'd like to pattern them like a quilt or maybe a stained-glass window idea, a picture within a picture."

"It's a small surface. When space is a factor, geometric patterns are more workable."

"So I'll do a small picture. Do I have time to play?"

"We never rush the wood." Brooks stepped back, satisfied and more than a little proud. "You play. If you need advice, give me a holler. If it gets busy up front, Tootsie and Ava will need you there."

"Got it. But in the meantime—" Liv held a tiny square aloft, squinting, her creative flair evident in her perusal "—I get to contemplate."

Her attitude reflected his. When you truly loved what you did, the job was never work. It was art, form, expression, joy, but not work. Not really. And on Saturdays he tried to be on the sales floor as much as possible, knowing his presence linked people to him, his business, his furniture, his craft.

And that made for happy customers. Happy customers became repeat customers. Never a bad thing because he really, truly enjoyed being paid for a job well done.

But Liv's revelation had offered another piece to Rita's puzzle, why she tried so hard to please her mother. Perfection was a hard standard to live up to.

He thought of his mother, her relaxed air, their home, full of fun, love and laughter. She never minded a crowd of guys around, the fridge stocked, cookies and cakes part of daily existence and everyone putting their feet up on the coffee table when they watched football, almost like an unwritten rule.

How ironic that he now lived a no-frills existence, with none of the small comforts that make a house a home, and that Rita had done her own about-face, leaving her mother's untouchable perfection behind and embracing a more carefree existence once Tom was gone and she was sober.

Much like his mother.

The analogy paused him. Mom would love Rita.

That thought illustrated how one mirrored the other in their focus, their humor, their decision to live life to the full.

I have come that they might have life, and live it to the full. The words from John's gospel pinched hard.

Isn't this exactly what Brooks removed himself from? Life to the full? Hadn't he sequestered himself to protect himself from that very thing, avoiding family, relationships, church?

And here Rita was, embracing it, much more newly sober, striving, working, juggling, managing. She was willing to push for her goals while he'd let himself become content just being.

But not anymore. Not in her presence.

"Brooks?"

"Yes, Liv?" He headed into the workroom and eyed the beginnings of her design. Soft blue and yellow tiles interspersed with ivory and a hint of dark green along the edges. "If I cut them the way I see them up here—" Liv pointed to her head and grinned "—I think I can come up with a look that totally says 'summer.'"

The pale yellow and deep sky blue did just that, the eggshell ivory a hint of cloud cover on an otherwise bright summer's day. He grinned. "I see it."

"Really?"

"Absolutely. Go for it."

She nodded, pleased. "I will. And you don't mind me cutting these? I'm not all that good yet."

"The only way to get good is to practice."

"Mom says that, too."

"Well, then." He smiled. "It's always good to agree with mothers."

"Sage advice."

Rita's voice drew their attention to the door. Her soft, blond hair swung forward, refusing her commands to stay behind her ears, and her expression said...

What? That she enjoyed seeing them working together? The pleased look on her face offered that and maybe a little more. Or maybe Brooks was hoping for a little more.

Pathetic, Harriman.

But it didn't feel pathetic. It felt good. Downright wonderful. For just a moment they were a unit, a family, and then Brooks remembered Callahan's phone call and recalled he'd had a family once and he'd abandoned them when things got rough.

Rita didn't deserve that and her kids had been through the wringer already. No more.

She moved forward, oblivious, the swing of hair making her sigh as she thrust it back, the gesture impatient. "Liv, this will be lovely."

"You think?" Liv's face brightened at this second voice of approval.

"I know." Rita leaned in and trailed her fingers against the tile, her face reflective. "They feel soft and hard at once. How is that even possible?"

"The smooth finish," Brooks told her. "It slips beneath your fingers and your head registers both senses of touch."

She gave him an over-the-shoulder smile that almost brought him to his knees. So sweet. So warm. So open. "That's why, really? How do you know all this stuff?"

He stepped forward, drawn but not wanting to be, pulled and unwilling to resist the warmth of magnetism. "Same way you understand the differences between white, yellow and silver cakes. I see vanilla, you see the real cake within."

"Now that makes sense."

"What brings you here this morning?"

"Brett had practice, Skeeter's at gymnastics, Liv's here and

I've done four applications so far and thought I'd run these specs by you to make sure I'm on target."

He looked over her figures and nodded. "They look good to me. Which banks did you apply to?"

She spouted off four names with local offices then added, "I'm doing as you suggested, too, and checking out the more distant banks with online applications. After you told me about that, I remembered my last car loan was out of a bank in Minnesota. They came in with the lowest interest rate, so I went with them."

"The Internet has taken banking competition to unprecedented levels."

"Well, we'll see." She shrugged as if convincing herself that the applications weren't all that important, just another step in an elongated process.

Brooks knew better but played along. "Do you have time for tea?"

Rita shook her head. "I wish I did. I have to get Skeeter in forty minutes and then be in Potsdam to pick up Brett and drop him off at Sarah and Craig's. He's working there this weekend."

"And this afternoon?"

She considered that and him. "What did you have in mind?"

"I need your vision for the bakery," he explained. "In order to get going on the basic carpentry, I have to see what works for you through a baker's eyes. Kitchens aren't exactly universal."

"Good point. But what if it's all for nothing? What if I don't get the loan?"

"I have to upgrade anyway. I've sent in the grant paperwork so it won't even be all my own money in the end, and since I have the time to get started, we might as well. If it's calm enough here this afternoon," he added. "And I'm totally optimistic that this will get funded, so why not get on with it now, while I've got time?"

"That makes sense."

Brooks grinned, hands splayed, his self-confidence obvious

and more than a little overdone at her expense. "Of course it does."

"I'm here, Boss."

Mick came in through the back, his backpack slung over one shoulder. He smiled at Liv and nodded Rita's way. "My exam was far too easy for the price I paid for the class, but it's over and I'm done for the next few weeks until summer classes start. Rita, great outfit. Didn't I see that on Jenny Stilson not too long ago?"

Rita burst out laughing. "Possibly. I always wonder if people will recognize their old clothes when I wear them around town."

"New to You will have a heyday of business with you working right next door," Brooks noted.

"If the bakery works out and I do well, I might not have to shop at consignment stores and Goodwill." Rita ran a hand across the three-quarter sleeve cotton sweater and shrugged. "But for right now, I'm not afraid to dress on a dime."

"And dress well."

She turned, smiling at his compliment, and Brooks felt that same tug to his heart. He did his best to tuck it aside.

No use. The smile, the lack of guile, her willingness to embrace her circumstances without belaboring life's inequities...

Wonderful. Amazing. Marvelous.

"So." He eyed the wall clock. "Can we meet around five?"

"Five-thirty," she told him. "And I'll have something ready for supper so we can all eat together later. If that's okay?"

Brooks loved food, especially food that didn't come from a can. Or the grocer's freezer. "It's a deal."

He almost said "date," again, but caught himself, then wondered why he did. Why shouldn't he date Rita? Take her out?

She'd put him off by reminding him they couldn't afford any more mistakes, an accurate assessment. Logical. Forthright.

But he didn't feel logical around Rita. He felt...invigorated. Hopeful. Almost young.

Which was totally ridiculous because he'd seen more by age

thirty than most men see in a lifetime, experiences running the gamut from horrid to awe inspiring. War offered an array of opportunities, good and bad.

My peace I leave with you....

Christ proclaimed peace and unity. Healing. Forgiveness. If Brooks were half the man he pretended to be, he'd have made peace with his family long ago.

My peace I give to you. I do not give to you as the world gives. Let not your heart be troubled and be not afraid.

"Earth to Brooks? Tootsie's calling your name."

"She is?" He stepped back, dipped his chin and smiled at Rita, tucking thoughts of John's gospel aside. "Five-thirty. You want to meet me in Canton or come here and we can drive over together? Or I can pick you up."

"I'll meet you there."

"Think about what will work best for you in the meantime," he told her as he headed for the showroom, Rita following. "Styles of shelves, cabinetry, space requirements for ovens, cooling racks, carts for moving product from the kitchen to the sales floor."

"I'll have a list ready and we can go from there. I've got the dimensions from the manufacturer's Web sites for the equipment I'll need, so we can plan around that."

"Good. Five-thirty."

She smiled, the warmth of her blue eyes made a touch deeper by the Columbia blue of the cotton sweater. It was a good look for her, casual, country and quietly understated. Much like the woman who wore it. "I'll be there."

Working with her on the specs for the bakery meant missing a meeting, but Brooks couldn't deny the spark of anticipation running through him.

An evening with Rita.

Sweet.

Chapter Thirteen

Seeing Tootsie that morning reminded Rita that Brooks was still in the dark about her condition. Before too long, Tootsie wouldn't be able to hide that she was pregnant, but Rita knew it wasn't her place to press. Still, she didn't want Brooks blindsided. Tootsie's due date put her firmly out of the mix for the holiday fourth-quarter rush, a mainstay of retail business. Rita decided to talk with her the next time they got a moment alone. Maybe she'd even stop by Tootsie's apartment. That way they'd be assured of privacy. Skeeter's voice yanked her back to the present, the wheedling tone that had become a regular irritant.

"Mom, Norrie's on the phone. She wants me to come over. Can I?"

"May I," Rita corrected for the gazillionth time.

Skeeter rolled her eyes, cocked a hip and assumed a bored expression. "May I?"

Saying the words hurt, but Rita read the body language. The sassy tilt of her daughter's head and the jutted hip spoke silent and plain: I'll placate Mom to get my way but no way will I pretend to like it.

But Rita was adamant about sticking to the plan. Brett was at Sarah and Craig's, Liv was working the day at the wood shop and loving it—perfect time for continued implementation of her plans for her youngest daughter. No more keeping the peace, praying for change. Oh, she'd still pray. The look on Skeeter's face ordained that.

But she'd stop shilly-shallying her way around an errant seven-year-old whose attitude needed big-time downsizing. "Is your room clean?"

Wide round blue eyes said Skeeter's room wasn't even close to clean.

Rita continued to fold laundry, keeping her manner light and her hands easy. "Tell Norrie you're still grounded for your behavior at Brooks' store the other night and that you can come over tomorrow as long as your room's done."

"But I want to go over today."

"Sorry. Next time behave yourself, okay? And your room isn't done in any case, so it's useless to argue. If you'd done it last weekend like I asked…"

"I did."

Rita shot her a look of disbelief. "You didn't, nor did you finish it during the week and now it's even messier. Start with your laundry. Bring anything that's dirty down here so I can wash it or you can put it in the hamper in the upstairs bathroom. Then put away your toys. You'll be ninety percent done by then."

"I have all day tomorrow," Skeeter whined. "Why can't I go to Norrie's now and do it then?"

"We're going to church in the morning and we've got company coming in the afternoon."

"Who?"

"Friends."

"You don't have any friends."

Ouch. Direct hit.

"Go. Now. Get it done or I'm taking away TV privileges for the coming week. Again."

Skeeter stared, looking ready to erupt.

Rita stared right back, chin up, shoulders back, brow drawn and eyes stern.

Skeeter caved.

Victory.

Small, sure, but Rita wasn't afraid to count even the small victories these days.

As Skeeter pounded up the stairs, Rita eyed the kitchen. She'd give it a quick once-over and then double-check her figures for Brooks. The guy was going out of his way to be generous with his time, funds and friendship. The least she could do was be prepared.

Quiet overhead told her Skeeter wasn't hustling to do her room, probably hoping Rita would stay downstairs and not make a fuss. She was half right. The fuss would come when Skeeter wanted to do something fun and Rita said no, instituting follow-through she should have used for years.

Better late than never.

She called up the stairs a little before five. "Skeets? Come on down. We've got to go."

"Go where?"

"I've got some business to do in Canton. How's your room?"

As if she didn't know.

"I'll do it tomorrow."

Drawing a deep breath, Rita inclined her head. "Then there's no TV, Skeets, not until you start cooperating. And no going to Norrie's either or any of your other friends until we have an attitude adjustment around here." Keeping Skeeter close at home probably punished Rita more than the kid, but that's how motherhood rolled sometimes. Just a little more often with this particular child.

Rita grabbed her bag, her folder, her pencil and headed for the door. "Come on. We've got to meet Mr. Harriman at his new store."

"What new store?"

Rita opted to keep her possible involvement on a need-to-know basis. Seven-year-olds could be put off, at least until the possibility of the bakery became a reality. "The new store he needs to do some work on. He needs our advice."

Skeeter groaned, grabbed her sneakers and headed to the car, muttering all the while.

Rita prayed for patience, stopped by the mailbox and grabbed the afternoon delivery. She leafed through the pile of letters with casual ease until the return address of one stood out.

Office of the Supreme Court, 48 Court Street, Canton, New York.

Sucking in a breath, Rita eyed the envelope, wondering, part of her wanting to rip it open while another part urged restraint, reminding her disappointments weigh hard on recovering alcoholics.

The first part won out. While Skeeter moped alongside the car, scuffing the toe of her new sneakers into the asphalt, Rita pulled the upper edge of the envelope open, mixed feelings flooding her. Fingers fumbling, she pulled out the judge's verdict with one hand while the other clutched the envelope. Pulling the folded papers open, her eyes scanned the contents until one sentence popped out from all the others.

"...it is the judgment of this court that the plaintiff, Rita Barnes Slocum, be given full access and custody of her share of the contested combined pension fund in the amount of no less than one hundred, seventeen thousand and twelve dollars and forty-two cents. Furthermore, the defendant, Edward R. Slocum, is instructed to pay all court costs in the amount determined by this court. Such funds as deemed necessary will be due to this court in thirty days from date of issuance."

Rita whooped, fist-pumped her delight, then sank to the ground, heart racing, quick tears filling her eyes.

"Mommy! What's wrong?" Concern for Rita chased the sullen look from Skeeter's face. She ran over and crouched by her mother's side, alarmed. "Are you okay?"

"Okay?" Rita laughed, cried and grabbed Skeeter in a huge embrace. "I'm more than okay, honey. I'm fine. Just fine."

Skeeter clung as though she never wanted to let go. "You're sure? You scared me when you fell down."

Rita waved the letter. "I didn't fall down, Skeets, I sat down real quick because I was surprised. And happy."

Skeeter's quick breaths began to slow down. "I like it when you're happy."

Of course she did, Rita realized. The kid had known nothing but conflict from the time she was able to walk. Rita nodded in understanding. "I do, too, but no one's happy all the time, Skeeter. This, however—" she waggled the letter between her fingers again, grinning down at Skeeter's bright blue eyes "—should hold me for a little while. It's a letter that says Uncle Ed has to give me your father's money."

"Why did Uncle Ed have Daddy's money?"

"A very good question, and one I can't answer, but the judge said he has to give it to me by noon on Tuesday. That's four days away."

"Can we get ice cream to celebrate?" Skeeter's expression turned optimistic and hopeful.

Rita tilted her head. "Is your room clean?"

A huge sigh. "No."

"If you clean it after church tomorrow, we'll go out for ice cream tomorrow night to celebrate, okay? But first the room gets cleaned."

"Okay."

Okay? Rita paused, amazed, then let it slide. Token appeasement wasn't unusual for Skeeter, but her agreement sounded almost sincere.

Wouldn't that make a good day just that much better?

Rita grinned, rose and tugged Skeeter along with her. "Come on, kid. We've got to get to Canton and start making plans for Mommy's new bakery."

"A bakery?"

"Mmm-hmm." Rita held the letter up once more. "One way or another we're about to make this thing happen."

Skeeter nodded, catching Rita's excitement. "Do I get to help?"

"As long as you're good."

Skeeter's countenance took on a softer air, more agreeable and confident than usual. "Then I'll try harder."

That in and of itself was a huge triumph in the motherhood

column. Yes, Rita wanted this baking dream to become reality. She had every confidence in her ability to tempt people with some of the best baked goods they'd ever tasted.

But more?

She longed for peace in her family, fellowship, normalcy. She wanted the American dream, the family of yesteryear working out their problems as they worshipped together, with children that loved and respected their mother. That would be a dream come true.

Chapter Fourteen

"**W**hat's up? What's going on?" Brooks sensed big change the moment he saw Rita's face, a hint of glee hidden behind a calm facade. The idea that she thought she could fool him after more than six years in special ops tweaked his sense of humor, but he fought the grin and let her play the part. "Are you okay?"

Skeeter's mischievous smirk only added to the comedy routine. Skeeter rarely smiled and never in his presence, an unspoken rule between them. He breathed, she scowled.

"Mom got a letter."

"Hush, you."

Brooks eyed them both, thrust a brow up, folded his arms and tried to look anxious, playing along. "Bad news, Reet? Is everything all right?"

Rita's poor attempt at constraint caved under his concern. "Look what I just pulled out of the old mailbox, Brooksie."

"Brooksie?" He half growled the nickname, sent her a pained look, took the letter, than laughed out loud. "This is some pretty good news right here."

"Isn't it?" Rita laughed, her face glowing, eyes bright, that swatch of disobedient hair masking her cheek. She thrust it back in an impatient move and nodded to the vacant store surrounding them. "Now we can get this done."

Brooks held up a cautioning hand. "Whoa. You're not thinking of using this money for the bakery, are you?"

"Of course." The look she gave him smacked of surprise. "It'll give us a good start-up base."

Brooks shook his head. "Can we talk about this now or will you get mad at me and stomp away and then come back later, ready to listen and apologize for going off the deep end?"

Rita wrinkled her face, dismayed. "I do that, don't I?"

"Yes. And it's actually cute sometimes."

"Ha, ha." She perched on the edge of a window seat while Skeeter wandered the store, examining the fixtures. "So, why shouldn't we use this to get started?"

"Several reasons. First, it's a pension fund so you'll pay big taxes on whatever you use early. If it's necessary to dip into it then the tax penalty is outweighed, but why give your money away needlessly?"

"But what if we need it?"

"Oh, we need it." He nodded, matter-of-fact. "For financial backing. This gives you solid backup money in the bank to augment your loan applications. It shows you're more financially secure and able to face a temporary slowdown of business if necessary. To open a new business you should have six months' cash on hand, ready to meet the demands of the business should anything happen."

He was right. Rita had learned that while procuring her business degree in Albany, but it seemed moot until now since she'd been broke for years. "So we bank this?"

"Most of it."

"And you think this will help my standing with the banks?"

"I know it will. Lending institutions don't want you to fail. If you lose, they lose. New equipment becomes used equipment the minute you plug it in, so their risk factor is highest initially."

"I'll amend the applications I already sent in." Rita nodded, thinking out loud. "And I got two more done so I'll readjust those figures and overnight them to the banks I'm targeting."

"Perfect." He reached out and pulled her into a hug, an

embrace that felt so nice she wished he'd never let go. "I didn't mean to rain on your parade, you know. Sorry."

She shook her head against his chest, loving the feel of his arms around her, his chin tucked to her hair. "No, it makes perfect sense and nothing I didn't know already. I was just a little giddy."

"A little?"

"Okay, a lot." She peeked up at him and saw the warmth in his eyes, a hint of humor, a measure of regard. Brooks was a steadfast guy, the kind that never played games. That regard was hard-won, something to cherish once given.

He eased back but didn't quite let her go, his right arm hugging her shoulders. "Have you got facts and figures for me so I can get a vision of what I need to do?"

"I do."

"Good." He gave her shoulder a light squeeze, pressed a gentle kiss to her temple and then released her, seeming totally unaffected by the hug and friendly peck of a kiss while her heart fluttered visions of happily ever after in front of her eyes.

Whoa, girl. Settle down.

Rita pushed the voice aside, allowing nothing to dampen her spirits. For this moment, things were going well, moving forward the way she'd hoped and dreamed. Sure, life would supply its share of smackdowns, that was expected in the real world. But she was better, stronger, wiser. She'd enjoy today's victory for the well-deserved moment it offered.

Rita took Skeeter's hand and headed for the back of the store. Brooks followed, his reading glasses adjusted low so he could focus on what she showed him and the notebook in his hand.

He looked adorable, but she didn't dare tell him so. An old soldier like Brooks probably didn't see adorable as complimentary, but the sandy hair, pushed back, always rumpled, the hint of gray at the temple, the rugged planes of his face and the unframed reading glasses...

Yup. Adorable.

She laid out the specs for him wall by wall, heights, depths, shelving, carts, etc. He nodded and jotted, eyes narrowed, asking pertinent questions when necessary, noting sizes and sketching a simple pictorial. Once done in the back, they moved to the front.

Rita waved a hand. "While I need utilitarian back there—" she motioned toward the kitchen "—out here we want North Country homey. Warm. Inviting. Reds, greens, golds and ivories. Over here—" she moved to the centered triple window, its view of Main Street ideal for Rita's vision, the small rectangles of glass offering invitation for seasonal displays "—I want the window seat offset so we can do displays along both the seat and the window. And we need the oven vent to go to the front of the building. If we take it out the top, that's fine, but then we want a deflector to push the scents downward, toward the sidewalk."

"Enticing people in."

"Exactly. What tempts the nose, tempts the wallet."

He grinned. "Yes, it does. Have I mentioned I love this slightly mercenary side of you?"

"Not as yet, but I'm happy to hear it," she quipped back, trying not to trip over her words. He hadn't said "I love you." He'd said he loved that side of her, a new facet previously unseen.

And that was all he meant, no doubt.

Which was good, because no way was she in any position to entertain thoughts of romance. She fingered the chip in her pocket, remembering her downfall and the work it took to achieve an even keel again. She could no more afford a tumble off the wagon than he could, and broken hearts were a barstool waiting to happen, so no. She absolutely, positively, indisputably was not interested.

Then why did his words spike her senses?

Because she was drawn to him, but who wouldn't be? Brooks Harriman exuded a strength and honor few people possessed and here he was, helping her, guiding her, laughing with her. Who wouldn't be attracted to that?

On top of that, Skeeter was behaving. For just a moment Rita thought she might be dreaming all this. But there was

Brooks, tall and strong, waiting for her to continue, looking too wonderful for her own good.

"So, tables here?"

His voice prodded her out of her daydream. She nodded. "Yes. Not too many, but enough for people to hang out since we have the room. Most bakeries don't. So we're double blessed that this location spread out in back allowing us more room to use in the front."

"Absolutely." He gave a firm nod, chin set, eyes twinkling.

"You're laughing at me."

He shook his head, smiling. "Not at all. I'm proud of you. A lot of people wouldn't have realized what a great decision Horace made by buying the back section of Higby's when they needed to downsize. His decision then makes your business more amenable now. You get the room for a full bakery and coffee bar because of a decision Horace made forty years back. Pretty cool that you saw that."

She quirked a brow, more than a little pleased at his confidence in her. "Thank you, Brooks."

"You're welcome, ma'am. Now, if we've got the basics done here, I'm starving and Skeeter's been wonderful through all this. How about we pick Liv up and head someplace for dinner?"

Skeeter shot him a look of surprise, then softened it with a little-girl smile, reminding Rita of what a sweet kid she'd been a few years before. "I promised you supper, remember?"

"But you've been busy." He nodded toward the court papers and Skeeter. "And I'd be honored to take you guys out to celebrate."

A tempting offer, but...

There was still the matter of a dirty bedroom at home.

Rita shook her head but passed a comforting palm across Skeeter's head. "How about tomorrow night? Skeet can't go out tonight because she's got to clean her room, but if she gets it done tomorrow, we could celebrate then. Would that be okay? My treat, of course."

Brooks slanted her a look that said no way, no how would it be her treat, but nodded approval at her tactics. "That sounds fine. Then we can all go together, especially if Brett's done at the farm."

"I'll let Sarah know. That way he can finish up and have time to get cleaned up before we go out."

"Perfect."

They headed for the door, Skeeter between them, her left hand in Rita's. As they stepped down, Brooks reached back and took Skeeter's other hand, then swung her down the steps in a fatherlike gesture, her eyes going wide as she swung through the air. "Gotcha."

She laughed up at him, joy replacing the customary sulking. "That was fun."

He squeezed her fingers lightly. "You were supergood in there. Thank you."

Skeeter dimpled, a hint of pride brightening her eyes. "You're welcome, Brooks."

His look softened as he regarded the little girl, probably the first time he'd seen the real Skeeter, the sweet child that lived beneath the surface snippiness. Rita longed to draw that child out again, give Skeeter reasons to shuck the attitude and draw water joyfully.

Speaking of which…

"We're going to the ten o'clock service at Holy Trinity tomorrow morning, Brooks. Sarah and Craig are bringing Brett with them. Would you like to come with us? Then Liv can go on to the wood shop with you."

"No, thanks."

No hint of hesitation, not a moment's thought. Just a simple refusal that said so much.

The little glimmer of what-if hope winked out inside Rita.

She'd pledged that she'd never settle for anything less than the dream again. She understood that not everyone who went to church lived their faith. Hadn't Tom gone religiously while he bilked members of their congregation and their town out of their hard-earned money? You'd never know it to see him sitting there in pew three each and every Sunday, chin up or head bowed, the vision of sanctity, all for show.

Whereas Brooks lived his faith in his simple kindness, his direct assessment, his helping hands, never looking for payment in return. His good works spoke volumes, the hands of a carpenter, tried and true, trusting and trusted.

But still a man who refused to go to church and worshipped on his own, a singular being, allowing no one in.

Rita wanted, no, *needed,* that community support. The feeling of being an accepted part of a whole, worshipping side by side with others.

She dipped her chin and nodded, then pasted a smile in place and headed for her car. "Well, there's a pot of meatballs and sauce ready and waiting at my place and I stopped to get bread at Shetler's Amish stand."

Brooks eyed her, seeing more than she wanted but she'd become accustomed to that. His keen eye wasn't easily fooled. He knew he'd disappointed her. What's more, he knew why. It showed in his quiet gaze, the set of his jaw. He squeezed Skeeter's hand one more time, nodded to Rita and headed for his truck. "It sounds wonderful, Reet. I'll pick up Liv and head over."

"Do you like garlic bread?" she called to him.

The grin that warmed his features warmed her heart right along with it despite her forced detachment. "Love it."

She smiled back but stepped away from the grin. She'd promised herself no more compromises, no more trade-offs, not of something that serious.

Where two or three are gathered in my name… Christ's words, his promise, his pledge, revealed in Matthew's tender gospel, the Lord's promise to be in their midst, walk with them, dwell amongst them. Sweet, sweet words, a boon to the spirit, a blessing to the heart.

Rita wanted that, hook, line and sinker. The warmth of a church family, church doings, festivities, services, bake sales.

All of it.

Brooks' quiet but firm rebuff said his goals, his dreams, his aspirations lay elsewhere.

She climbed into her car, gave him a friendly wave, complimented Skeeter's behavior yet again and headed home, the mix of feelings palpable within her heart.

Chapter Fifteen

He'd blown it big-time. The moment he uttered the rejection and read her expression, he realized he'd gone one step forward only to move two steps back.

Or more.

Most likely more.

Liv and Tootsie were still cashing out, giving him time to ponder his words at length, the empty parking lot a reminder that most people shared their Saturday evenings at home, with family.

Would it be so hard to go to church with them? Sit in a pew, praise God with others? He'd done it occasionally since moving north, a wedding here, a funeral there.

And each time, he'd pictured Paul's face on the minister, maintaining a front to his congregation while sleeping with his brother's girl.

His soldier brother's girl.

The soldier brother risking his life in a war zone, while Paul slept with his future sister-in-law.

Brooks scrubbed a hand through his hair, kneaded his neck and wasn't sure if he wanted to growl or sigh.

He still couldn't block those visions of Paul and Amy every time he heard a minister prattle about sin and temptation. Could he do it for Rita?

He pinched the bridge of his nose, wishing he could, knowing

he couldn't. Not now, anyway, with Callahan's news so fresh in
his head.

Go home, an inner voice scolded. An inner voice that sound-
ed more than a little like Rita. *Make peace with your brother.
You grace perfect strangers with your warmth and humility.
Shouldn't you do the same for your own brother?*

Yes. Absolutely. Positively.

That was it in a nutshell. He needed to see Paul. Seek forgiveness. Offer forgiveness. Move on.

But with all Paul and Amy were facing right now, was it the
right thing to do or was it a selfish eleventh-hour act, concern
for cleansing his sin, his soul, before Paul's untimely death? And
in honest appraisal, did he deserve forgiveness for abandoning
them? Turning his back? Refusing contact?

Brooks saw the sin on both sides. Was he man enough to do
something about it?

A movement drew his attention toward the rear of the store,
near his apartment door. Nothing furtive, just a flash of red-
gold, a glimpse of something.

Should he ease the truck across the lot or check this out on
foot?

Walking, he decided. He climbed out of the truck, curios-
ity pushing him forward, caution moderating his approach.
He left the truck door ajar to avoid making noise. Careful, he
eased around the corner of the store, alert and maybe a touch
on guard.

The dog lay alongside the building, curled against the basement blocks as if seeking their support. In the oblique light of
late day, the quiet animal glowed with a hint of etherealism, a
trick of the sun, no doubt. Brooks approached slowly, sensing
trouble, the garbage hound's reluctance to run totally out of
character.

Brooks hesitated, uncertain, wanting to make sure the pooch
was all right. "Hey, pal."

No growl. That was good, right?

Brooks crouched low. "How we doin'?"

A tired thump offered a meager greeting from a dog usually

quick and energetic. And smarter than Brooks ever thought of being.

"You hungry? Thirsty? Need a place to chill?"

The dog thumped his tail, and sighed as if relieved to be understood after all this time.

When I was hungry, you fed me. When I thirsted, you gave me drink....

Brooks wasn't sure it counted with dogs, but no matter. He couldn't leave this poor, tired animal without some sort of comfort, a place to lay his weary head as the evening temperature dropped into the upper thirties.

"Hey, Boss, what are you skulking around over here for?" Liv and Toots came around the corner, more than a little curious.

Brooks put a finger to his mouth and jerked his head toward the dog.

Liv and Tootsie charged forth, crooning and cooing, their combined voices a melody of love, first approaching the dog, then petting, patting, rubbing his head, his side, his belly.

"Do you see tags?" Brooks asked.

Liv massaged the dog's neck. "No."

"Collar?"

"Nope."

"Hmm."

"He's thin," Liv noted. With the glow of youth that feared little, she seized the dog's face between her hands and examined the dog's eyes, mouth and ears. "His coat's not only dirty, it's dull. A stray or abandoned, most likely. This is the guy that's been keeping you up at night?"

"The very same."

"Well, he's gorgeous. Or he would be with a little TLC. But at the moment, he seems a little down."

"We can't just leave him here," Tootsie noted.

Brooks brightened. "You could use a dog, Toots. A woman alone. He could guard you against all kinds of things."

"In Grasse Bend? You're kidding, right? Besides, I'm here all the time, I can't be heading home to let a dog out midday. And my landlord would have a cow and raise my rent, neither of which makes my preferred list. But you, Boss." She raised a dark brow in his direction, slid her gaze to his apartment then back to the adjacent store. "You could easily take care of him right here."

Brooks backtracked. "He may not be a stray."

Liv eyed the dog and Brooks. "Um...right."

"He might have a home hereabouts."

"Where they don't feed him, bathe him, collar him or de-flea him."

Fleas? "I don't do fleas."

"Craig's got great stuff that kills them. You just put on a few drops each month and you never see a flea."

"And you know this because?" Brooks turned his attention to Liv, wondering why on earth they were even having this conversation. He didn't want or need a dog.

Did he?

He thought of the mischief the animal had already caused. His missing shoe, the garbage rummaged and strewed no small number of times.

The look of hunger in the dog's soft brown eyes sealed Brooks' fate, at least temporarily. He turned back to Liv. "We've got to call your mother, tell her we're running late."

"And him?" Liv nodded at the dog, lying on his side, seeming too tired to move.

"I'll call Craig. Have the old boy checked out."

The girls' combined smiles made him feel ten feet tall. If only life was always that simple, that easy. He called Craig, arranged to meet him at the vet clinic just a few blocks away, then hoisted the dog into the truck, the girls following in Tootsie's car.

They made an interesting entourage as Craig unlocked the clinic, his schooled look assessing the dog's condition before Brooks set the old guy down.

"Young."

Brooks sighed and scrabbled a hand through his hair. "Is he sick?"

Craig shrugged and looked as if he was biting back a smile,

but with his chin dipped it was hard to be certain. "We'll soon know."

Brooks nodded.

Liv took his hand and squeezed, somehow understanding that despite the dog's mischief, Brooks was worried.

Craig ran his hands along the dog's head and shoulders. When his fingers palpated the dog's side, the retriever whined. Craig paused, frowning, then probed gently again, studying the dog's pained reaction. "We've got some soreness here. Combining that with his lethargy suggests an HBC."

"A what?"

"Hit by car," Craig explained.

"Really?" Brooks leaned forward and stroked the dog's head. "Is he all right?"

Craig nodded. "I think so. He's showing mild signs of trauma and the soreness factor is pronounced. Probably why he didn't run off when you approached."

"Poor fellow."

"I'm going to keep him here, give him fluids, get him stabilized for overnight. We'll see how he's doing tomorrow. I expect some fluids, rest and food will put him to rights again."

"Brooks, I'll donate my paycheck this week to help cover his expenses," Liv offered.

"I can pitch in as well," Tootsie added. "Whatever it takes."

Brooks waved them off. "Even at Doc's inflated rates, I can handle this, girls, but thank you for offering. Well, hello." He smiled as Rita and Skeeter came in from the back door, the concern on their faces mirroring the rest of the room. "We didn't mean to hold you guys up."

"You didn't." Rita passed a hand over the dog's head, his ears. Skeeter followed suit. "We just couldn't stay away once Liv called. The sauce can be warmed up when we get back. How is he?" Rita looked up at Craig as he prepared an area for the stray animal.

"I think he'll be just fine with a little love and attention. Food, family, fun. That's what this boy needs." Craig scratched the dog behind the ears, grinned down at him and continued, "Between all of these guys, there should be at least one person to offer you a place to lay your head, young fella, if not more."

Liv sent Rita an imploring look.

Rita sent it right on to Brooks, a brow shifted up, her gaze encouraging and supportive.

Oh, man.

"I'll hang on to him until we find his owner."

Rita wrapped an arm around his waist and squeezed. "I was hoping you'd say that."

The scent of warm vanilla sugar cookies blended with vet hospital and dank dog, and Brooks zeroed in on the sweet vanilla, the warmth exuding from Rita's enthusiasm. "I don't really need a dog," he noted, musing. "But it appears to need me."

"Better yet," Rita declared. She grinned up at him and he found his heart tripping over itself to inspire that smile more often.

The dog whined again, a little softer this time, his voice relaxing as if knowing help was at hand.

"I'm going to tuck him in for the night. He'll be sequestered in the back kennel and then I'll meet you guys here after church in the morning, okay?"

"Fine." Rita nodded.

"I have to work but you guys can keep Toots and me posted, right?" Liv swept Brooks and her mother a look of inquiry.

"Sure." Rita shifted her attention to Brooks, one arm slung around Skeeter's shoulders while the little girl petted the dog, totally oblivious to the possibility of fleas, parasites, germs or any and all forms of vermin lying therein. Didn't they teach kids about such things at school anymore? Maybe not in first grade. Brooks hoped Craig's flea treatment worked as fast as they'd all promised.

"We'll meet you here, okay?"

Brooks nodded, drawn back into the flow of conversation. "Okay."

She didn't touch on the fact that he'd refused to meet her

at the church just a short time ago. No, she glossed right over that.

Smart woman.

Brooks reached out and sank his hand into the dog's ruff, deciding if the kid could risk it, so could he. "Hey, pal."

Thump, thump, thump.

"He likes you." Skeeter's exclamation was accompanied by a sweet smile of delight, total innocence and light.

"He seems to."

"Oh, he does," she promised. "He didn't thump like that when the rest of us petted him and when a dog thumps his tail, it means they like you and want you to pet them even more."

Brooks sent her a smile and kneaded the dog's neck again. "We don't want to disappoint him, do we?"

"Oh, no." She peered up at him, aghast. "And if you need help with him, I can come over."

"You can?" Brooks held back the heightened note of surprise, but shifted a brow up, wondering at Skeeter's promise, her cooperative attitude.

"You can?" Rita repeated, doubt in her tone. They both knew Brooks didn't rank real high on Skeeter's list of important people to impress. "You'd like to help Brooks with the dog?"

"Oh, yes. I'm good with animals. Aunt Sarah says so."

Craig nodded, not even trying to hide the grin now. "And Aunt Sarah is always right."

"Wise words from her husband," noted Brooks.

"I'm a smart man." Craig studied the hypodermic in his hand, nodded and injected the dog. "I'm administering rabies and distemper vaccines, just in case. He's neutered, so someone spent some time and money on him at one point."

"We'll watch the newspaper to see if anyone advertises they're looking for him." Brooks met Rita's eye.

Craig shrugged that off. "You can check, but the likelihood is slim."

"Even so, it would be wrong not to check."

"True enough."

They helped settle the dog into the back kennel. The young

retriever was asleep before they made it back down the hall into the surgical end of the veterinary clinic. "He'll rest well tonight. Plenty of food and water available."

"And the fleas?"

Craig grinned. "I administered a topical and I'll set you up with a dosing program. That way we can keep fleas and ticks controlled for however long he's with you."

Brooks nodded, then shook Craig's hand as they headed toward the door. "Thanks for coming out, interrupting your Saturday."

"A good cause," Craig assured him. "And I'm billing you for an emergency visit." At Brooks' wince, Craig grinned. "We need new computer upgrades and I've got to bring some impressive money in ASAP."

"Glad to help, Doc." There was no missing the wry note in Brooks' voice.

Rita smiled. So did Tootsie, Liv and Skeeter, all at him, their gazes reflecting warmth and pride.

His heart swelled like the Grinch overlooking Whoville, realizing that Christmas was more than presents. Brooks looked at Liv. "You can ride with me if you want. Or your mom."

She headed for his truck while Tootsie angled for her small sedan. "I'll ride with you. I love riding in trucks."

He turned back toward Rita. "Meet you at home?"

He meant her home, of course, but why did it feel so good to just imagine that? All of them, en masse, heading for home?

"I'll start the pasta water."

He climbed into the truck, bemused and a hint delighted, as if he'd taken a big step forward through no fault or design of his own.

He flicked his gaze upward, sent God a silent thumbs-up and started the engine, hoping the dog would be fine.

"So." Liv fiddled with the radio station, found a country station they both liked and settled into the seat as Rascal Flatts waxed poetic about broken roads. "How was the bakery meeting? Did you and Mom get it all worked out?"

"I'm starting work on it Monday."

"So soon?"

"Why wait?"

"But what if..." Liv hesitated, choosing her words.

Brooks understood. It's hard to ask one drunk what might throw another drunk off the wagon and be sensitive about it. He grinned. "You're wondering how to ask me if she's ready for this without hurting my feelings, right?"

She cringed, embarrassed. "Yes."

"No guarantees, Liv. Not now, not ever. But the good thing is, your mother is working hard every day to maintain an even keel and it gets easier as time goes on."

"But she could still crash."

"Yes. And most of us have done it a time or two, but then we climb back up, dust off our knees and get going again." He let his words settle before asking, "Do you talk to her about this?"

Liv shook her head. "Not much. I don't want to hurt her feelings or bring it all back up or push her over the edge."

"Brett said the same thing."

She stared out the window, pensive, then dipped her head in acknowledgment. "We talk about it sometimes. Not so much now."

"Because she's doing much better."

"Yes."

"Cling to that. And pray for her, even if praying isn't cool for your generation."

"I pray." Liv slanted a look his way. "For a while I prayed just to get by, you know?"

Oh, he knew, all right.

"Now..." Liv paused again, her forehead wrinkled, but her face serene. "Now I pray because I want to, I want things to go on the way they are. Calm. Peaceful."

"Amen."

She grinned.

They pulled up in front of Rita's home, lamp-lit from

within, the windows glowing at various levels, the porch light welcoming Liv home.

The contrast to his dark existence loomed.

Brooks never left a light on that wasn't being used. Waste not, want not, his years of frugal military existence filtering into civilian life even after all this time.

From a practical mind-set, he could scold about wasted money, the energy of all those lights very un-eco-friendly. But...

He liked the effect. The warmth exuding from the clean panes of glass, lace curtains diffusing the glow here and there. The homey look invited him to linger and that was something to celebrate after years of sadness.

Brooks climbed out of the truck and followed Liv up the walk, the lamplight bidding him entry. And for just a moment, one brief, little moment, Brooks felt as if he was coming home.

Chapter Sixteen

Rita pushed open the vet-clinic door after church and saw Craig and Brooks, chins down, deep in conversation, their stature spiking her worry for the dog. She moved forward quickly. "How's he doing?"

Her question drew their attention her way. Brooks' smile offered answer enough. "He looks better. Still quiet but not as pained."

When he stepped aside, Rita nodded in agreement; the dog's happy face was a testament to his improved health. "Much better, I'd say. Now how are we going to keep him in? And by 'we,' I mean 'you,' of course."

"But you said 'we' and Doc's a witness." Brooks grinned down at her, his face looking relaxed. Peaceful. Younger. "And that's a very good question. What do I do with him when I get him home?"

Craig ticked off a list. "Feed him, walk him, don't let him run in traffic and reapply the flea deterrent once a month."

"That's it?"

Craig shared a grin with Rita. "That's not even the half of it, but you're a smart man. You'll find your way. You've never owned a dog before?"

Brooks' hesitation shaded his features, then he shrugged. "When I was a kid in Baltimore. His name was Boog."

"An Orioles fan."

"You know your baseball, Doc." Brooks nodded appreciation. "We named him after Boog Powell, one of the best sluggers of our time."

Skeeter sidled in from where she'd been petting Craig's on-site cat. Rita had every intention of playing a trump card to inspire the kid to clean her room. Brooks didn't know it but his new pet had just become the treat rewarding the trick. In this case, the trick was a clean room.

The treat?

Helping Brooks with the dog.

Oblivious to her plan, he bent and gave the retriever a gentle head massage, steering clear of the dog's sore midsection. "Boog died when I was in high school and I haven't had a dog since."

"I'm sorry your dog died, Brooks."

Brooks gave Skeeter a look of gratitude mixed with something else. Understanding, maybe?

"Thanks, Skeeter."

"Can we take him home now, Uncle Craig?" Skeeter tilted her gaze up, eyes wide. "I bet he really wants to have a nice home."

Craig palmed her head. "He's good to go."

"I think my place is a little bare to be categorized as nice." Brooks turned Rita's way as if seeking assurance. Talk about a role reversal. "Should I even be doing this?"

"I'm going to tell you exactly what you'd tell me." She angled her head, set her jaw and met him eye-to-eye. "Stop wavering and just get on with it, for pity's sake. Yes, you should do it, the dog doesn't need, care for or want fancy rugs, furniture or dishes. Eating your smelly old shoe proved that."

A grin of remembrance relaxed Brooks' features.

"What he needs is someone to feed him, walk him, brush him and play with him. And clean up the yard after him."

"How fun."

Rita grinned. "We'll get some special little bags for just that purpose at the pet store."

"Are they open today?"

She nodded. "The one in Potsdam is and they encourage you to bring your dogs along."

"You're kidding."

"Nope."

"Can I come, too?" Skeeter edged forward, one hand kneading the retriever's fur, the other clutching her mother's hand. "Please?"

The moment of truth had arrived. "Is your room clean?"

The look of abject disappointment that grayed Skeeter's feature clutched Rita's heart. Even Brooks and Craig looked as if they wanted to cave.

"N-no."

Rita offered her an even gaze. "Then no. You can't. Maybe next time, if you get your chores done."

Skeeter gulped but didn't look as if she wanted to explode or implode, a big step up. She just looked sad.

Craig and Brooks exchanged looks of chagrin. Before either one of them could blow this teachable moment by caving and cajoling Rita to let Skeeter come, Skeeter took matters into her own hands. She sent a trusting look up to Brooks and moved to his side. "If I go home and clean my room right now, could I come with you later? I can work really fast when I want to."

Brooks looked to Rita for guidance. She gave a slight nod.

"You have to do a really good job. You know that, right?"

Skeeter nodded earnestly.

"And I haven't got all day." Brooks made a show of looking at his watch, one brow thrust up. "You'd need to be done by—"

Rita raised one finger behind Skeeter's back.

"One o'clock. Think you can do it?'"

Skeeter grasped his hand, clung tight and nodded, her pigtails bouncing. "I'm sure I can."

Rita awarded Brooks and Craig extra points for not laughing out loud, Skeeter's display of sincerity a wonderful rarity. "Then we better get home now, Skeets." Rita took Skeeter's other hand and for a sweet moment they were linked, Brooks, Skeeter and Rita, the dog holding center stage between them.

Brooks felt it, too. She knew that because he sought her gaze, his glance dipping to their joined hands, the dog, the feeling of family surrounding them. "Reet, can you call me, let me know if everything's okay to pick you girls up around one?"

"Of course."

Warmth flooded her with his look of approval, their shared smile.

Craig broke the moment by heading toward the back door. "I promised Sarah I'd be home in time to get the first coat of paint on the nursery."

Rita nudged him. "I can't wait for next month. A new baby, a brand new life." Seeing Brooks' nod prodded a quick feeling of guilt inside her, remembering Tootsie's news, her condition.

Knowing Brooks, she understood Tootsie's reticence. Brooks' approval was sought by many, a trait intrinsic to the man himself. Tootsie hated to disappoint him.

But knowing Brooks' understanding heart, Rita was certain it would all work out. Brooks showed that weekly by helping AA members, new and old, offering them humor, example and wisdom, very Ben Franklinish only way younger. And cuter.

That thought inspired Rita's grin.

Still, Tootsie needed to come clean. Before too long her pregnancy would be obvious and Brooks needed to be told before he guessed.

But for now, she had every intention of seizing the moment at hand, getting Skeeter home, out of her church clothes and focused on the promised task.

A clean bedroom. At last.

"So. What first, pal?"

The dog entered Brooks' apartment without a moment's hesitation, as if he'd known all along he belonged there and was just biding his time until Brooks figured it out.

Score another point for the canine.

The dog sniffed the perimeters, a puzzled look wrinkling his brow as he scented his way around the three rooms. Once done, he sat back on his haunches, eyed Brooks and tilted his head as if asking, "That's it?"

Brooks grinned, reached down and petted him. "Afraid so, pal. Kind of small, but you and I don't need much, do we?"

The dog's look said they'd discuss that at length later on, after a dish of food or something equally appropriate.

Brooks pulled out the saucepan he'd used on the porch and mixed up a similar stew to the one he'd offered days before. "After this, it's dog food for you, pal. Straight from the bag. Got it?"

A quick canine nod said the pooch understood completely but was imminently grateful for a cupboard stocked with canned soup. Since Brooks was altogether tired of eating canned soup, they worked out a deal.

Rita called just before twelve-thirty. "So far, so good," she whispered. "Call me back in ten minutes to see, okay?"

Brooks laughed. "Secret missions, a former specialty. Should we synchronize our watches?"

"You think this is funny? It's just about monumental."

Brooks eyed the newest member of the Harriman family and offered agreement. "I think we've both achieved milestones today. Your kid is behaving herself and the world at large is grateful for that…"

"Ha, ha."

"And I," he went on, ignoring her interruption, "am now a pet owner, a part of the American mainstream, a man with a purpose."

"It took a dog to give you purpose?"

"Let's just say the dog is representative of a growing purpose."

"Oh, my goodness, do you ever listen to yourself? Seriously?"

He laughed out loud. "Yes, and usually it makes me nauseous. If we don't end this call, I won't need to make another, we'll have used the ten minutes up. You realize that, don't you?"

"Goodbye."

"Talk to you in five."

"Dogs don't need beds." Brooks looked somewhat thunder-struck at the thought, brow furrowed, eyes narrowed. His glance at the price tag intensified the look, especially after he scanned the already full cart.

"You're right, of course." Rita nodded in agreement, as she headed down an adjacent aisle stocked with collars and leashes. "Why go to extremes? He can just share your bed." Eyeing rhinestone-studded raspberry collars, she laughed at Brooks' horrified expression and moved two steps down. "Whoa. Camo, in desert or jungle. What do you think? Does this guy remind you of a soldier?"

Brooks squatted to where Skeeter held tight to the leash Craig let them borrow. "What do you think, pal? Camo?"

The dog eyed both selections, a "you've got to be kidding" expression tweaking his demeanor.

"I thought dogs were color-blind."

"They are."

"Who decides that stuff, anyway? I mean, do they ask the dog? Have ink-spot tests of color? How do we know they're color-blind, or is this going to be like so many other things science is absolutely, positively sure of until they discover, oops, they were wrong?"

"It doesn't matter. I think Skeeter has a winner."

Skeeter held out a thick red nylon collar, the color a nice standout against the dog's russet tones. "He likes this one, Brooks."

Brooks rehung the camouflaged collars. "I think you're right. Let's try it on, see if it's the right size."

"It is." Skeeter's voice caroled enchantment as Brooks snapped the collar into place after adjusting the length. "It's perfect, Brooks."

"So it seems." Brooks smiled down at her, patted her head and then nodded to the wall display. "He'll need a leash to match, don't you think?"

"And a tie-out," Rita interjected.

Brooks hesitated.

Rita read the look and sighed out loud. "You can't bear to tie him outside, can you?"

"Possibly. Maybe. From time to time."

"What are you going to do with him while you're working?"

Brooks shrugged. "He can hang in the shop with me. In the workroom. As long as he doesn't mind the smells."

"You old softy."

He flushed. Really cute.

Rita grinned. "I wouldn't have believed it if I hadn't seen it with my own two eyes, Brooks Harriman."

"It makes perfect sense." His insistence only intensified her grin. "He needs company and a good dog is a deterrent to crime."

Rita swept the dog a look as he proceeded to lick a complete stranger's hand. "Absolutely. If someone breaks in through your state-of-the-art security system, the dog can lick him to death."

"I'll consider him a security-enhancement device," Brooks agreed. "That way he becomes a tax deduction."

Rita rolled her eyes as they added the leash to the cart. "Does he have a name yet? Because at some time we need to stop calling him 'dog.'"

"I don't know." Brooks bent again, rubbing the dog's head and jowls, his light eyes meeting the dog's darker gaze. "What do you think, pal? What sort of name would you like?"

"What about Pal?" Skeeter peered up at Brooks, her expression thoughtful. "That's what you always call him and a dog is a pal, right?"

"Once again, I'm in total accord." Brooks met Skeeter's gaze and felt another corner of his heart melt under her innocent scrutiny. "Pal it is. Thank you, Miss Skeeter."

She beamed, the smile finishing the day's transformation, the sweet child within released for a while at least. First last night, now this afternoon...

Whatever Rita was doing appeared to be helping. Brooks wasn't afraid to offer a silent prayer that the progress continued. A peaceful Skeeter made a world of difference to the family dynamics. He saw that by simply assessing his own reaction, the ability to relax and not cringe in her presence.

"So. Are we set here?"

Rita scanned the list and the cart. "Yes. Your mission, should you choose to accept it, is to break out your credit card and pay the bill." When he gave an exaggerated cringe, she leaned closer. "To help avoid cardiac arrest when the clerk hits Total, just envision an even bigger tax deduction."

He bristled on purpose and pointed to Skeeter. "She's a tax deduction and no one finds that disturbing or mercenary."

"Personal tax deductions are a totally different matter. Everybody knows that."

He grinned down at her, loving the repartee, the teasing, the laughter Rita inspired.

Loving her.

The realization jolted him initially, then settled in, like the feeling of a warm, dry towel after a brisk swim, comforting him, a gift of solace and solidarity.

The moment hung between them, gazes locked, awareness spiking, the fun, family-oriented jocularity evolving into something more, something sweet and inviting, enticing them into untested territory. Stepping closer, Brooks allowed the feeling to cloak him, comfort him, Rita's pretty smile an invitation to linger.

She recovered first.

"We're all set, right?"

He sent her a lazy grin that allowed the quick change while sending a promise of more to come.

She swallowed hard, tucked her chin and headed toward the checkout counter with decided purpose, her quick steps making Skeeter skip to keep up, Pal trotting alongside.

"He likes to run, Brooks."

Brooks remembered Pal's middle-of-the-night raids. "Yes, he does. And he's looking more chipper today, isn't he?"

"Much," Skeeter offered, eyes bright, tone upbeat, a wonderful, marvelous thing regardless of cause. "I think he's doing better because he knows he's found a home."

Funny, Brooks was just thinking the same thing about himself, how much better he felt being in Rita's company, sharing her open approach to life and laughter, her slapdash, first-things-first mentality. Seeing Skeeter's step-by-step transformation, he was beginning to see that with God, all things were possible.

His cell phone rang. He scanned the display and frowned.

Rita stepped closer. "What's up?"

"It's Jeff. Trouble." Brooks sponsored Jeff Reddings, a local farmer who fell into an alcoholic heap after too many years of rough weather and crop failures. Jeff wasn't a newbie to AA; he had several chips to prove his dedication to sobriety. If he was asking for help, immediacy was important.

"You go."

"But what about—" Brooks motioned a hand to the dog, the cart, the checkout girl.

"Give me your card. It's no big deal, Brooks."

He moved forward, cradled her cheeks with two big, strong, wonderful hands and gave her a quick kiss on the mouth.

Too quick.

He touched his forehead to hers, whispered "thank you" and headed out the door at a quick clip.

Then turned right back around, realizing she and Skeeter had no way home if he took the truck.

Rita waved her cell phone at him. "I'm calling Craig. Go."

The look he sent her said more than words, more than the kiss. It was a gentle look of love, of gratitude, of thanksgiving.

She gave him a grin, waved and tried not to think of the dangers inherent in falling in love with Brooks Harriman.

Too late.

Were they foolish, downright silly or crazy to be considering a relationship?

All of the above. Still…

Thoughts of his warmth, his slow, easy, heart-stopping grin, that almost-always-irritating steady look of appraisal, which so often turned out to be right.

An infuriating trait for sure.

But those hands, big and brawny, tender around her. Wielding the wood, placing tile, caressing the dog. Before you know it she'd be standing in line, waiting for a pat on the head.

"Mom? She needs money."

Chagrined, Rita offered the card, signed Brooks' name and pushed the cart to the door.

"Why did Brooks leave us here alone?"

Rita stooped down. "A friend of ours from AA needed him. He's Brooks' special friend and Brooks made a promise to help him whenever he needs it. So when he called, Brooks had to go."

"Without us?"

Rita nodded matter-of-factly. "Yup. Sometimes when grown-ups have problems they need a chance to talk about it with other grown-ups."

Skeeter's features darkened, as if the conversation brought up a bad memory. "Do you still have problems, Mommy?"

Rita refused to lie. "Yes, but I'm working hard to handle them. Just like I want you to do."

"What do you do when they get too hard?"

A loaded question with a simple answer. "I pray. I pray real hard."

Skeeter sighed, her look way too worldly for a seven-year-old. "I tried that. It didn't work."

Mixed emotions flooded Rita. She didn't miss the humor in a seven-year-old waxing dramatic about unanswered prayer, but the look in Skeeter's eyes said more. "Don't give up, Skeets. And if you need help or advice, I'm here."

For a brief moment, Skeeter looked tempted, then shook her head. "I'm okay."

Craig's SUV pulled up out front a few minutes later.

Rita gave Skeeter a swift hug, then petted the patient dog's head. "We'll take this stuff to Brooks' place, get Pal settled and go from there, okay?"

Skeeter kneaded the dog's silky coat, her growing affection evident. "Or we could take him home with us."

And then Brooks would have to come by to pick up his dog. Rita grinned. Tempting but…

"Pal needs to get acclimated to Brooks' house, his schedule. That means he has to get used to things over there. If Brooks has to be gone a long time, we'll drive back over and take Pal for a walk, okay?"

"Okay."

"Let me help you with that, Reet." Craig hoisted the dog food while Skeeter and Pal climbed into the backseat.

"His seat belt doesn't fit because he won't sit still."

Rita finished unloading the cart and ducked her head into the car. "Dogs don't wear seat belts."

"But what if we get in an accident?" inquired Skeeter, incredulous. "He could get hurt, right, Uncle Craig?"

Craig hid a smile. "You're absolutely right so I'm going to drive supercareful, okay?"

That mollified her, as if it was okay for Craig to not drive supercareful with mere humans aboard. "Thank you."

"You're most welcome." He sifted his gaze to Rita. "Brooks had to leave?"

"A call."

"Ah."

Craig wasn't one to nose around in other people's business, a quality Rita admired. He thrust the car into gear and headed for the road. "We're stopping at his place first?"

"If you've got time."

He nodded. "You caught me just as I finished the first coat of paint, and my wonderful nephew is home helping my pregnant wife inoculate a barn full of dim-witted, wool-bearing animals…"

Rita laughed. Craig had never been a fan of sheep. Shepherds? Well, when the shepherd looked like Sarah Slocum, Rita's sister-in-law, that was a whole different story.

"And a new boxful of baby Maremmas."

"Oh, he'll love that," Rita noted. Brett loved dogs, and working on Sarah's farm afforded him growing skills. He was becoming quite adept at hand commands and whistles, skills Sarah used with ease. "Is this Lili's litter?"

"Yes. Sophia's due in two weeks."

"Oh, my."

"Exactly. I'm grateful Brett likes being there, helping out.

With all the work of spring planting and the flurry of lambs, Sarah's moved through this pregnancy with lightning speed."

"Never a bad thing," Rita observed. "I'm still surprised you didn't want to find out if it's a boy or a girl."

Craig shook his head, smiled at the sight of Skeeter petting the dog in the rearview mirror, then flashed a quick grimace to Rita. "I wanted to. Sarah just laughed. Says she's waited all her life for this surprise and refuses to be cheated out of it by technological wonders."

"Sounds like Sarah."

"It does." Craig's expression belied the wry tone. He'd fallen head over heels in love with Sarah, despite her ardent attempts to thwart his enthusiasm, thinking herself unworthy. Tom's legacy of crime and deceit had made things tough on a lot of people, Sarah among them.

"Have you picked out names?"

Craig nodded. "McKenna if it's a girl."

"I love that name. McKenna Macklin. Perfect."

He smiled. "We do, too. And if it's a boy, he'll be William James for my grandfather. We'll call him Will."

That name made Rita sigh.

Craig's grandfather had been one of Tom's victims, a good man whose hard-earned money disappeared in Tom's hands, leaving him and Craig's aged grandmother penniless, dependent on others in their old age. And here was Craig, her friend, her brother-in-law of sorts, ready to help with whatever proved necessary. Such a good man.

"A beautiful legacy."

Craig nodded and sent her a look that said he understood. "Yes, it is."

Chapter Seventeen

Brooks winced as he pulled into Jeff's driveway off County Road 7. The farmhouse carried an air of abject neglect, its splotched facade worn thin like overbleached cotton. With Jeff's successful years of recovery, Brooks hadn't been out this way in a long while. Too long, it seemed.

He parked the truck and strode up the walk, wishing Jeff had said he needed help and understanding why he didn't. Pride could trip a man more often than not. Jeff's predicament showcased a perfect example. Brooks ran the bell and waited, impatient, shifting his weight and working his jaw.

But when Jeff opened the door, Brooks presented the stance of a friend, stoic and stalwart, ready to listen. Share. Whatever it took to stave Jeff's urge to drown his sorrows on a barstool. Brooks grabbed him in a guy hug, then stepped back, concerned. "What's going on?"

"Wendy left."

Jeff sat on the edge of a living room chair and motioned Brooks to do likewise with a wave of his hand. The clatter of little feet above announced the presence of kids. Jeff jutted his chin toward the stairs, acknowledging the noise. "She left me a note saying she couldn't handle all this." Jeff waved his hand toward the noise of the kids playing upstairs and then the house, not nearly as forlorn inside as it appeared outside, "Said if I got a real job, we'd never have fallen on hard times."

"Ouch."

"Yeah. Trouble is, she's right."

Brooks knew she wasn't. He understood that Jeff was born to the land and that bad luck could happen to anyone. But right now Jeff *felt* as if Wendy was right and that's what Brooks played to. "Farming's tough."

"Yes."

"Long days, long nights."

"And not much money to compensate for those."

"Not nearly as much as there should be. Had she talked about leaving before?"

Jeff shifted his jaw and angled his gaze on the window. "Off and on. I didn't pay much attention because she'd only say it when she went off the deep end about something. Work. The kids. The schedule she has to keep. I mean, that's what mothers do, isn't it, Brooks?"

"What exactly?"

Jeff stood, paced and shrugged, running a hand through his hair. "Take care of things. The house. The kids. Running them around, taking care of them, getting their stuff."

Brooks digested the wrongness of Jeff's appraisal.

His growing ties to Rita and her kids had him seeing things through a whole different light. "So Wendy worked full-time at the clinic, took charge of the house, the laundry, the shopping, the kids, and ran taxi service for whatever they needed to do while you farmed."

Jeff met Brooks' gaze and recombed his fingers through his hair. "Basically."

"Are your bills paid up-to-date?"

Jeff nodded as though that were a given. "Yes."

"And the kids are healthy?"

"Yes."

"And you love her."

Jeff's eyes misted. "Yes. I'm such a jerk."

Brooks sat back. "Yes, you are, but you're not a bad jerk. Just a chauvinistic jerk. And there is help for men like me and you."

Jeff eyed him. "You? A chauvinist? Mr. Nice Guy?"

"A nice guy who just saw the light through your eyes and realizes it takes a lot to make a husband and father. Way more than a paycheck."

"And when those are somewhat choppy, season to season..." Jeff's voice wandered off. "I should have done more."

"Most likely."

"Helped."

"I'm sure she would have appreciated it," Brooks replied. "Guys our age are kind of caught in between. We grew up with the idea of women's work and men's work, so we weren't raised to do this naturally. But it's not fair to slough all that off on a woman when they're working an outside job to help pay the bills."

"It's tough when my life is on a tractor six months of the year."

"And I bet she'd understand that if you were more help the other six."

Guilt rode roughshod all over Jeff's face. "You're right."

"So go after her. Where is she?"

"At a friend's."

"Call her." Brooks nodded to the phone across the room. "Don't say anything major on the phone, other than an apology and a declaration of your undying love. Just ask to meet with her. Talk with her."

"And if she refuses?"

"You suck it up and try again tomorrow. And the next day. And the next. You do whatever it takes, man."

Words of wisdom, spoke from the heart of a man that needed to take his own advice. So be it.

Two little boys clattered down the stairs. Brooks sprawled on the floor with them, racing tiny metal cars around and around the weave of the rose-toned braid rug covering nicely finished hardwood floors. The boys' energy level offered support to Brooks' conclusion. Wendy needed another fully invested adult on hand, the sooner the better. Of course a year or two of good harvests and strong milk production wouldn't hurt things, either. Sufficient funds provided a great equalizer.

Jeff came back from the kitchen after a short conversation. Brooks read his face. Better. Much better. He arched a brow of question.

"We're meeting tomorrow afternoon, once she's done working."

"Here?"

Jeff shook his head. "No. At the park. I'm going to drop the boys at my sister's place after school and meet her. She wanted someplace private and we used to go walking along the old trails before the boys were born."

"You okay?" Brooks' pointed look added more to the question.

"Yes. Yes, I'm fine. I just needed to talk, to have someone tell me it will be all right."

"And it will, one way or another."

Jeff eyed the boys as a toy truck wreaked havoc on an unsuspecting bright red convertible. "Whatever happens, they need me sober."

"Amen."

Jeff reached out a hand. "Thanks for interrupting your Sunday, man."

"No thanks needed. Keep me informed?"

"Will do."

As he pulled out of the driveway, Brooks made a note to organize a painting party for the Reddings come the dog days of summer. No matter what happened, the outside of the house could use a fresh look and the porch planks needed a thorough sanding and refinishing, all things a crew from AA could handle.

Pal's happy bark greeted him at the door, and Brooks grinned in reply, rubbed the dog's head and took him outside for a quick turn around the yard. As he watched the dog prance, Brooks withdrew his cell phone and dialed Greg Callahan's number.

He'd told Jeff to do whatever it takes. Now he needed to

drum up the guts to follow his own advice. Greg answered on the second ring.

"It's about time, Captain."

"I know. How's he doing?"

"Holding his own for the moment."

Brooks sighed. "I've got to finish up a project here. It will take a few days."

"Days you've got. Weeks, maybe. Months? Not so much."

"I understand." Pal returned to Brooks' side, panting a second welcome, his happy face an expression of unequivocal love. Brooks returned the smile as he stroked the dog's fur. "I'll call when I've got things in order."

"I'll be here."

Brooks disconnected, eyed his austere apartment and headed for the truck with Pal, knowing Mick, Liv and Tootsie had the store well in hand. "Come on, boy. Let's go where the action is."

Pal rode shotgun as if he'd been born in a truck, ears perked, chin high, his stance saying he was ready for anything.

Brooks read the dog's profile and wished he could say the same about himself.

The sound of Brooks' truck brought Rita outside, concern for Jeff increasing her speed. "How's Jeff doing?"

"We got through this one. Some rough stuff going on but hopefully they can work things out."

"Marriage stuff."

"Yes."

"That's tough."

"So it would seem."

Something in his voice, his bearing, drew Rita forward. "You've never been married?"

He stared at a nearby copse of evergreen before pulling his gaze back to hers. "No."

"Engaged? Fallen in love?"

Regret washed over his features. "Engaged, yes. A long time ago."

"She broke your heart."

He acknowledged that with a nod and a sideways glance. "Partially. The other part being I was young and stupid."

Rita reached out a hand to his arm, seeing the pain that had hovered too long. "We were all young and stupid once, big guy. But I'm sorry."

"I was, too. Now?" Brooks swept his gaze around, his eyes blanketing the trees, the small town neighborhood, the purr of traffic at the nearby intersection. "Not so much. Still, there are things I need to fix."

"Such as?"

The squeak of the screen door interrupted. "Mom?"

Pal raced ahead, tail upright, his enthusiasm for Skeeter reflected in the child's face as she bent to his level, which wasn't all that much different from hers. "Hey, Pal. How are you doing?"

The dog sat, prim and proper, quivering with delight as she stroked his head. Skeeter handed Rita the phone. "For you, Mom."

"Thanks." Rita moved a few steps away, her expression waxing from quizzical to disbelieving in short seconds. "You're serious?"

Brooks and Skeeter edged her way.

She waved them off. "Yes, of course. I'll check for the e-mail and the attachments right now. Are you sure this is real? It's not some scam?"

The loan officer on the other end of the phone laughed. "No, ma'am. I work Sundays now and again to stay up on things. Today was one of those days. When I received the update about your upgraded financial status, it was enough to move you into the yes column."

"Thank you."

"You're welcome. If you could download and print those papers, get them signed and notarized and overnight them back to the address in the e-mail, we can direct deposit the funds into your account ASAP."

For the past weeks she'd wondered if she was doing the

right thing, taking this chance. She'd prayed and planned, but still doubted. Right now those doubts floated away on a cloud of euphoria inspired by the bank officer's phone call. "I'll get right on it."

She disconnected, turned and let out a whoop, fist-pumping success. "I got it!"

"What?"

"The loan."

Brooks laughed out loud, hugged her, spun her around, then hugged Skeeter and at least half of the dog. "You're sure?"

"Reasonably certain. We should find an e-mail from Andronia Savings and Loan inside with all the necessary papers attached."

"Interest rate?"

"I'm falling under the umbrella of a federal program that offers help to women in business, so the interest is 3.8%."

"That's wonderful. Let's go see if that e-mail's there, get things in motion."

She hesitated, looking up, studying him. "We were talking."

"Yes." He rubbed his neck, indecisive, then jerked his head toward Skeeter. "We'll finish later."

"Okay." She didn't like that choice, knowing Brooks, but Skeeter's presence limited their current options. So be it. She headed inside and turned toward the kitchen alcove, anxious to see if that phone call was genuine. Minutes later, she sat back, pleased and surprised. "It's for real, although I'm still having a hard time processing the whole thing, especially on a Sunday. Doesn't anyone take a day of rest anymore?"

"You snooze, you lose. Obviously this loan officer weighed risk versus gain and you measured up."

"You think it's a bona fide acceptance?" She printed off the response and held it out for Brooks' perusal.

Brooks read the e-mail as Rita printed the attachments, then cocked his jaw, nodding, probably having no clue how endearing that expression had become. Of course that was mostly because she'd allowed herself to fall over-the-top in love with a guy who kept his past to himself and avoided church at all costs. What on earth was she thinking?

That he was one of the kindest, gentlest, most honest men she'd ever met?

With a previously unknown penchant for dogs. He must have read her bemusement because his expression sparked humor in the crinkles surrounding those deep gray eyes. "It's done, Reet. You got it."

"Unbelievable."

Concern washed over him as she sank into the nearby chair and burst into tears for too many reasons to count.

"Hey. Hey."

"I'm okay." She waved a hand in his general direction as she blubbered into a kitchen towel that had seen better days.

"Of course you are." Brooks sent a baffled look to Skeeter as she came through the swinging door separating the kitchen from the living room.

Indignation, worry and protectiveness combined to make Skeeter's scowl quite convincing, reminding Brooks her improved behavior might be short-lived. "Did you hurt her?"

"Never," Brooks promised, then wondered if he had the right to make a promise like that. He'd hurt his family and did nothing to make amends.

Taste and see the goodness of the Lord.

Beautiful words of faith, of taking that step forward.

"Then what's wrong?" Skeeter edged forward, uncertain.

Rita swiped the towel across her eyes, reached out and hugged Skeeter. "I'm crying because I'm happy."

"Huh?"

Brooks bent to Skeeter's level. "My sentiments exactly. I don't try to figure it out, I just go with the flow."

"But you're okay?" Skeeter pressed.

Rita pushed up, hugged her and gave a brisk nod, remembering the chip in her pocket, the mandate she strove to live every day. *Change the things you can...* Wasn't that exactly what she was doing? *Yes.* "I'm more than okay. I'm wonderful."

She flashed Brooks a smile that thanked him for his caring, his friendship, his support and maybe more.

"This makes our celebration tonight doubly sweet."

"It does."

"And when we get home we can process orders for equipment and supplies and make lists of what needs to be done."

"And a whole bunch of us to help," he reminded her.

She absorbed that, nodded and took a deep breath. "You're right."

His raised hands, half shrug and smug expression wondered why she might have expected anything else.

She sent him a dour look, his chronic self-confidence almost cute. Almost. "We can combine forces and see what's what, who's available to help with furniture, cleaning, buying." She sailed into his arms and hugged him, holding tight, feeling more right and natural than he had hoped and dreamed for years. "Thank you."

"For what?"

Her smile said more than words ever could. "Everything."

His heart burst wide open, embracing her, her family, her lick-and-a-promise housekeeping. Holding her, cherishing her, this was the future he'd wanted and needed without knowing it.

Including the dog.

But God knew. He'd planted her in front of Brooks, brought her out of the realm of insanity and into the sweetness of life, a second chance, a new opportunity for both of them.

Skeeter sidled in and Brooks reached an arm around her, grateful for the two days of improvement he'd witnessed. Whatever the little girl's problems might be, she was working to correct them, a big step forward.

Rita planted a kiss on his cheek, a peck of a kiss that said thank you and nothing more, but enough to let him know he wasn't all that off base in his hopes and dreams. Her sweet rise of color added depth to his supposition. "I've got to call Kim."

"She'll be thrilled. Her mother was better today, but she can always use good news."

Rita's grin made him cross his arms and lean against the kitchen counter while she talked, his expression curious, while Skeeter led Pal outside.

"Kim? It's Rita. No, no, everything is fine, just fine. And Brooks said your mom is improving."

"She is." Relief softened Kim's tone, but she was never afraid to share her true feelings with Rita. "And I try not to fool myself about this whole thing, the mess of no job, Mom's health, the insurance snafus with her, but I'm not a stay-at-home kind of person and it's driving me bonkers, Rita."

"Sooo…" Rita hesitated long enough to draw out her point. "How would you like a job?"

"A job? What are you talking about?"

Brooks grinned approval, realization dawning.

"I just got the loan approval for funds to open my own bakery in Canton and I can't think of anyone else I'd like to have run it with me. I can't pay a whole lot initially, but I think we'd enjoy working together and I need someone I can trust, who doesn't mind getting up early and who understands the way I do things."

"Rita, I don't know what to say." Kim sounded overwhelmed and flabbergasted, but more than a hint elated. "Are you for real? The loan's a sure thing? We can really do this?"

"Can and will. So. What do you say? Are you on board?"

"Kimberly Anna Pappas Nikolas, at your service. And don't think I won't bring some of Mama's and Yaya's recipes along. Yaya's baklava was absolutely amazing, so melt-in-your-mouth good."

"Perfect." Rita met Brooks' smile and returned it. "You go back to taking care of your mom and we'll get everything in order here. If all goes well, we could possibly be open by…" Rita scanned the calendar, then shifted a brow to Brooks.

"June first. It's a Saturday. We'll open then, close for Sunday and Monday to regroup, then reopen on Tuesday."

She beamed. "That soon? Really? Are you that good?"

Brooks grinned. "No, but my friends are."

Kim laughed, overhearing. "Count me in. Oh, Rita, I don't know how to thank you."

As if. Kim had been a mainstay in her life for over a year now, a true blessing. "No thanks needed, you know that. I'm absolutely, positively, wonderfully excited. I'm going to let you go, clean up and take Brooks and this family out to dinner."

Kim laughed. "Go. Have fun. I'll talk to you tomorrow. But, Rita, in all seriousness? Thank you."

Rita breathed deep, understanding the silent message of friendship. "You're welcome."

Brooks stepped forward once she hung up the phone. "You're an amazing woman, Rita.

She dipped her chin, flushing.

He tipped it right back up, the callused feel of his thumb tender against her throat. Did he feel the quick beat of her heart, how the flutter of her pulse ramped up whenever he was near?

His smile said yes. The sweet kiss confirmed it, the press of his mouth tender and firm, strong and gentle. He drew back, dipped his forehead to hers and sighed. "Pretty sweet day."

She laughed. "I'd say. A dog and a loan. Wonderful."

"While I was referring to the kiss."

She blushed.

He grinned. "But the rest was pretty nice, too."

"Brooks, I—"

He stepped back, winked, then nodded toward Pal in the backyard. "If we're going out, I need to get my dog home and get changed. I'll be back in an hour, okay?" His look of appreciation told her words weren't necessary, that he understood all her heart wanted to say.

She smiled and grazed a hand against his cheek. "We'll be ready."

Chapter Eighteen

Brett walked into the bakery site late the next afternoon and whistled softly. Brooks interpreted his look and smiled.

"I must have missed where Ty Pennington came on board for this project," he told Brooks. "Did you get the entire crew of *Extreme Home Makeover* in here today?" Brett made the observation as he stepped forward, his incredulous look asking how Brooks got so much done in so little time.

Brooks laughed. "A bunch of AA guys came by first thing this morning and we busted loose."

"I guess. The wall, the cabinetry, the shelf space."

"And that was after we upgraded the electric, coaxed the building inspector to come by and check it out because we needed his stamp of approval before we could proceed and then reran plumbing lines to the sinks, dishwasher and bathroom."

"Wow."

"Yeah." Brooks set down the molding he'd just triangulated to fit an outside corner abutting the ceiling and nodded to the front. "I'm having you redo these walls tonight."

"With?"

"Paint, first." Brooks nodded to carefully unboxed panels leaning against the side wall. "Then wainscoting tomorrow."

"How do you know how to do all this stuff? Did you go to school for it?" Looking more than a little amazed, Brett swung back and trained his gaze on Brooks.

"My dad does fine carpentry in Baltimore."

"He taught you?"

"The same way I'm going to teach you," Brooks told him. Thoughts of working alongside his father, emulating Bill Harriman's even demeanor, reminded Brooks of what his father believed and embraced, what a strong man like that stood for.

Honesty. Integrity. Forgiveness. And more than a little grit thrown in on the side.

"Let's get you set up with the sander." Brooks handed the small power tool to Brett.

"Can do." Brett settled in to work, quiet and focused, great qualities in an adolescent. By the time Rita came in, Brett had completely sanded the upper walls and set up sawhorses in the kitchen area to apply the first coat of paint to the sales-area moldings.

"I can't believe how much you got done." Rita spun in a circle, then shook her head. "How did you do this?"

"Little elves in a hollow tree?"

He sent her the smile that melted her resistance a little more every time. After all, not all Christians went to church, right? A lot of people lived their faith quietly, out of the mainstream. Would it be so horrible for Brooks to worship in his own way, his own time?

In the end, what was worse? A man like Tom who attended in name only or a true believer like Brooks Harriman, a man whose life testified his faith commitment.

But you wanted normal, the inner voice insisted, refusing to be quelled by fairy-tale thoughts of romance and ever afters. *You promised yourself you'd never settle again.*

Would loving Brooks be considered settling?

No. But a relationship needed total commitment on both sides, and important matters like faith and children shouldn't be downplayed, ever.

"You up for a dirty job?"

Brooks' query yanked her attention to the here and now. She flushed inside and out, ruing her telltale skin and the emotions banked just beneath the surface. "I'm in. What's the job and how do I do it?"

Brooks pointed at the floor. "Tile removal. We have to get the old floor off before we can put the new floor on."

"That doesn't look too hard." Rita eyed the tiles, unfazed. "Some of them are already chipped and loose."

"And some aren't." Brooks tossed her a wide-blade putty knife. "Give it your best shot. I'll join you when I'm done here."

"Okay." Earnestly she tugged on plastic gloves and dived into the job with all the vigor of someone who's never pried old tiles loose before. Three minutes later, she lifted her first linoleum square, sticky black residue clinging to the underside. "Got it."

Brooks glanced at his watch, made a face and surveyed the floor. "At three minutes per tile, we won't be ready to open by Labor Day, much less June first."

"Ha, ha."

"Are they really that tight or are you that slow?"

"I'm a girl, remember?"

He set the moldings aside and moved up front to help her. "It'll go faster if we work together," he said in answer to her questioning look. "It's always easier with two, and once you get a rhythm going, the tiles come up better."

"Oh. Well. Good."

"Have you talked with Kim today?"

"Twice." Rita flashed him a grin but kept right on working, unintimidated by the dust, dirt and physical labor. "She's psyched."

"That was a nice thing you did, offering her the job."

"Not nice. Necessary."

"She's got no experience and a sick mother."

Rita shrugged that off. "She loves to bake and takes direction well with a perfectionist's eye to detail. Since I tend to fall short in that arena, we make a nice balance."

"So you'll train her."

"Kim's smart. It won't be all that difficult. It's more learning the routine than the actual baking for lots of things. And she actually taught herself how to decorate cakes, so I'll leave the simpler ones to her."

"I'm still proud of you."

A flush climbed to her cheeks as another linoleum square hit the growing pile.

"You made a move like that when it would have probably felt safer to find someone experienced with commercial baking. It took guts."

"No guts, no glory, soldier."

Soldier.

At some point he had to open up to her, tell her about his life in the service. And about Amy and Paul. How he left them all high and dry, hightailing it out of there for dear life. Not much heroism there. He'd been on the verge yesterday until the bank officer called.

"We're almost done."

He nodded. "We make a good team, Reet."

She slanted her gaze over to him, her pretty blue eyes the shade of an August sky along the shore. "You think?"

Gulp. "I know."

"Well, that's good since we've developed an ongoing work relationship."

Brett's voice interrupted whatever comeback Brooks might have entertained. "You guys getting hungry out there?"

"Starving."

"Pizza?"

"Anything." Rita looked up as Brett came through the door. She nodded toward the window seat. "My cell phone's in my purse if you want to call in an order."

Brett jutted his chin toward the door. "DiGuardi's is three stores down. I'll walk over."

"That's so nice of him," Rita noted as she shifted her focus back to the tiles.

"Uh-huh."

Something in his tone brought her head around. "It wasn't nice?"

"Let's just say that altruism isn't Brett's only motivation for walking over to order pizza."

"An ulterior motive? Such as?"

"Casey DiGuardi?"

"A girl."

"Yes."

"But just last year he thought girls were yucky."

"Not anymore."

Rita digested that information, shrugged and nodded. "I'll have a chat with him like I did with Liv a few years back. Do boys like to talk about this stuff?"

Brooks hoped his horrified expression underscored his words. "Not on your life."

Rita put heart and soul into a melodramatic sigh. "Brooks, it *is* okay to talk about things. Some consider it normal."

"Not when it comes to boys, girls and adolescence," he shot back. "We don't talk, we observe, then hope we get it right. Eventually. After years of practice. Possibly decades."

"Brooks."

"Trust me on this. If he wants to open up or ask questions, he will. Otherwise—" he put a finger to his lips "—shh."

"I'm his mother. It's my job to invade his privacy. And since you take the strong, silent mind-set to the extreme, you might just be wrong."

"Don't say I didn't warn you."

Rita rolled her eyes then shifted to the next row of tiles. Was Brooks right? She had no idea, but if Brett's growth spurt meant he was entertaining ideas in directions other than soccer and farms, she'd have to broach the subject.

Watching Brooks' steady progress across the floor, she couldn't help but think how nice it would be to have his input with Brett, the example of a fine man for her son to follow.

Brett and Craig got along great and Brett's job at the farm kept them in frequent contact, but Rita refused to pretend that was the same as having a hands-on dad day after day. Since Tom had fallen way short in that department, her kids had been shortchanged.

But taking on three kids was no picnic, even without their combined addiction. With their alcoholism thrown into the mix?

A combustible blend, for sure.

Rita's cell phone rang as they finished up. She answered with one eye on the clock, knowing they should have cleaned up an hour before. She'd given her two-week notice at the commercial bakery but her boss was on vacation, the assistant manager had come down with late-season influenza and they had a corporate challenge this week to benefit cancer research, a huge deal in their grocery chain. Rita needed to be on her game the next four days to pull off the baking schedule required to keep their displays filled and inviting.

"Mom? It's Liv. Skeeter's got a fever."

"Oh, no. How high?"

"One-oh-two."

Brooks moved closer, realizing something was wrong.

"I've got acetaminophen in the medicine cabinet, Liv. She gets two teaspoons."

"I just gave it to her. But she's definitely not feeling good. I've got career-planning day at school tomorrow, so it's no biggie if I miss that, but then I start prep for final exams."

"Maybe she'll be better by Wednesday." As a mother, Rita understood the unlikelihood of that but clung to the hope.

"Norrie has strep. Her brother told me this morning."

Skeeter hadn't caught the strep virus in two years, but when she did, the bug put a nasty hold on her. "We're on our way, Liv."

She hung up the phone and turned toward Brooks and Brett, who had returned with the pizza. "Skeeter's sick."

"So I gathered. Bad?" Concern hovered in Brooks' gaze, his eyes shadowed.

"Maybe strep. Liv's staying home with her tomorrow and I can get her into the urgent-care facility now."

"Really?" Brooks glanced up at the clock, amazed.

"They're open till eleven. But it's a tough week at work with the corporate challenge and all, so I don't know what to do about Wednesday. Or Thursday, if necessary."

"Leave her with me."

Rita eyed Brooks with a mix of hope and trepidation. "You won't throttle her?"

Brooks and Brett both laughed out loud. "I can't promise that," Brooks replied, "but she's definitely been better the past few days. And how naughty can she be when she's sick?"

"This is Skeeter we're talking about," Rita warned. "And you two haven't exactly gotten along in the past."

"But we have Pal now." The dog was a huge check in the points-gained column. "We'll be fine," Brooks insisted. "Wednesdays are notoriously slow at the store and you can finish your work schedule without feeling guilty or losing money." He moved closer. "Do you need help with her tonight?"

Such a tempting offer. Skeeter wasn't exactly an easy patient. Oh, no. Being sick only heightened her less stellar qualities.

And while her forty-eight hours of better behavior was worth celebrating, Rita'd been a mother long enough to understand illness could topple the best of intentions. "Thanks, but no. We'll be fine."

Regret deepened Brooks' crow's-feet but he accepted her refusal, understanding. "I'll check with you tomorrow, but if she's not going to school on Wednesday, I'll pick her up before Brett and Liv get on the bus. Tell her to bring along anything she needs. Toys. Games." He took a deep breath and almost choked. "Dolls."

Rita smiled over her shoulder as she hurried to her car out back. "Will do. And Brooks?" She dipped her chin toward the store, the upgrades, the work he'd thrown himself and half their friends into. "Thank you."

"My pleasure, ma'am."

Chapter Nineteen

"This smells bad." Skeeter offered her whiny pronouncement as they made their way through the shop to Brooks' home.

Since it did, he nodded. "Your sister likes the smells."

"She's stupid."

Obviously Skeeter hadn't forgiven Liv for going to school. Brooks let the comment slide. "Come through here, Skeets. I've got everything ready."

She sniffed audibly as she stepped through the door to his apartment. He raised a brow. "Better?"

"A little."

Pal padded across the room to offer Skeeter a warm welcome, his tail wagging with delight. The dog's presence softened her woebegone expression.

But not her attitude.

"Where's the bathroom?"

Important information. He showed the little girl around the apartment, then set her up with ginger ale and crackers once she refused breakfast. Flicking the television on, he tossed her the remote. "You know how to use this?"

"I'm seven."

Right. He bit back words of reprimand at her tone. One step at a time, he reminded himself. He recalled the intense training the army provided its special operatives, hoping to toughen them should they ever be held hostage, providing them with the resiliency needed to survive enemy captivity.

Gain their trust. Stay low-key. Noncombative. What worked for the army ought to work on a seven-year-old in Grasse Bend, New York.

He hoped.

"We're fine, so far," he reported to Rita a few hours later. "We've played old maid, go fish and countless games of memory. Hasn't anyone thought to teach her solitaire?"

Rita laughed. "Wearing you out, is she? Don't you have to get over to the store?"

"Yes. I'll head next door, get things going with Tootsie, then come back to check on her. There's no fever, no flushing. Just tired and irritable."

Rita's voice reflected dismay and maternal guilt. "You're sure you're okay? She's okay?"

"We're fine. Want to talk to her?" Brooks moved across the room, offering the receiver to Skeets.

"Sure."

Skeeter refused the phone. "I'm busy."

"It's your mother." Brooks eyed her, then dropped his chin. "She wants to make sure you're all right."

"She should have thought of that before she left." Eyes down, Skeeter snapped the taut response just loud enough for Rita to hear.

Brooks fought the dressing-down he wanted to dish out. Not his place. He heard Rita's sigh and turned his attention back to her. "Sorry."

"Don't be." Her tone was plaintive. "We'll bring her around. Bit by bit."

Brooks eyed the kid and realized he was too old-fashioned for today's parenting techniques. He'd have laid down the law long ago, letting Miss Skeeter know her attitude better change in quickstep time or she'd lose privileges until they did. Privileges like food. Sustenance. Oxygen.

The thought inspired a wry smile that was part grimace. It

was easy for him to be stern. He wasn't carrying the guilt Rita did around her shoulders. The same guilt that pushed her to whiskey short years ago. He drew a breath and kept his voice warm. "Call me later, when you have time."

"Will do."

After opening the store, he checked on Skeeter. Tootsie and Ava had arrived to run the sales area and Mick was working on shelves for an antique-style step-back cupboard. Seeing Skeeter sound asleep, Brooks marveled at the innocence of her expression in slumber. He breathed a sigh of relief and decided to do some scrollwork he'd put aside.

Lost in his work, Brooks glanced at his watch and stood abruptly. Nearly two hours had passed. He uttered a silent prayer that she might still be sleeping. The blare of his computer system killed that thought as he stepped through the door.

"What in the world?"

Simply put, he needed to throttle her. Sure, she was a kid, but no jury would convict him if they saw the ribald images flashing across his computer monitor. How had she—?

He kept his voice level with effort. "What have you done?"

"I didn't mean to." The magnitude of her mistake shook Skeeter's peevishness. "I wanted to play computer games and you didn't come back so I tried it out. I clicked on the Internet and all this stuff showed up."

Oh, man. Swiping a hand through his hair, he scrubbed it across the back of his neck. "I don't believe this." Brooks approached the system, his brain sorting through the myriad of things she could have messed up or destroyed with a click of the mouse. He closed the offensive images, leaving the room suddenly quiet.

"I'm sorry."

Her voice wasn't bratty or abrasive. More like terrorized. He turned to face her and was startled by the look of abject fear. As he stepped forward, she moved back, cowering, the dog at her side.

His heart wrenched. The urge to strangle her disappeared in a heartbeat. Instead, he held out his hand. "Come here."

She did because there was no other choice. He led her back to the computer chair, Pal trotting alongside. Fighting a groan, he settled himself into the seat, then hoisted her onto his lap, feeling her heart race. "Let's see if we can fix this, okay?"

She nodded, silent. With a few deft strokes, Brooks trashed the offensive Web site, then deleted the inevitable cookies accompanying it. Once he had a clear view of his desktop, he slid the mouse in front of her. "Try this instead," he offered, feeling her stiffen.

"But…" Temerity laced her voice, fear of repeating her mistake quelling her normal behavior. With good reason, Brooks mused, wondering how he'd explain this to Rita. He sighed. He'd figure that our later. Right now…

"Right-click here," he told her, pointing to an icon. "We'll see what's in cyberspace for kids, okay?"

They found all kinds of things on the Web, some good, some not so good. Brooks wouldn't let her linger on kids' sites lacking a good message. "Why would a fifteen-year-old wear that kind of makeup?" he growled as they checked a popular singer's home page. "Or those clothes? Nope, that one's off-limits, Skeets. Let's see if there's a better site."

She didn't argue. Not one peep. Maybe sparing her life had bonded them. Once he had her firmly ensconced in the antics of a singing cucumber and tomato duo, he started a quick lunch of grilled cheese and tomato soup, then called Rita to confess.

"I don't know how she managed to get to that kind of site," he babbled. "I don't have stuff like that on my computer, Rita. I really don't."

Rita's crisp response offered reassurance. "One of Brett's friends sent him a music file they both wanted. He downloaded it and e-mailed it to Brett. When they opened it, this 'special edition' song was filled with X-rated material. It's everywhere, Brooks. Besides, she couldn't have seen too much, could she? With you right there?"

"I was in the shop." He had no intention of downplaying his

neglectfulness. "I went over while she was sleeping and lost track of time. If I'd been here like I was supposed to be…"

"It wouldn't have happened," Rita agreed, but she didn't sound condemning. She sounded…understanding? Empathetic? "Welcome to parenthood, Brooks. Murphy's Law. Anything that can go wrong, will, and at the worst possible time."

"You're not mad?"

"Did you strangle her?"

"What? No. I thought of it," he acknowledged, flipping the grilled cheese. "But she was scared. I figured the best thing to do was to show her how to use it correctly, after I got over the urge to lock her in the dungeon."

A smile skipped across Skeeter's features. She was listening, although her eyes were trained on the vegetable medley in front of her, fully aware he was shouldering his share of the blame. "Gotta go. Our lunch is ready. Bring home something for dessert tonight," he added as he poured creamy red soup into matching bowls.

Rita's voice held a smile. "I will."

He loved her, heart and soul. If he thought it before, he knew it now. He'd messed up his duties and she forgave him, not expecting perfection. Another space nudged open inside, a hollowness he'd kept closed away.

Operators needed to be as perfect as possible to pull off their missions. Synchronization was huge and adaptability more so. Real life didn't offer the same strict parameters. As he set out the food, he understood that was why he'd kept himself on the edge of life so long. Lack of control scared him, both his and others.

Rita had opened those doors. Her belief in him, her own neediness and now her growing strength had him almost believing he had what it took to make a future with her. Forge a family. Then again, his track record there was less than sterling. Sighing, he said grace, surprised this parenting thing wasn't as simple as he thought.

"This is really good." Skeeter nodded in approval as she chewed a bite of sandwich.

"My mom used to make it for me when I was a kid." Brooks dipped his sandwich into the soup before taking a bite. "It's my favorite lunch."

"She's a really good cook, then," asserted Skeeter, following suit. "My mom is a good cook, too."

"She is." Brooks nodded in agreement. "She's sorry she doesn't have more time to cook right now, with her job and the work on the new bakery."

"I just miss her."

Brooks read between the lines. Being sick equated with wanting Mommy. Understandable enough.

"I can teach you how to make this yourself," Brooks promised. He didn't feel guilty that the soup was canned and the sandwich a two-minute quick fix. At seven years old, it was haute cuisine.

"I'd like that."

Brooks smiled. "Me, too."

Weariness reclaimed Skeeter by midafternoon. Brooks straightened the covers and settled her in with her well-worn teddy. Noting her heavy lids, he smiled and dropped a kiss on her brow. "Sleep tight, munchkin."

He started to move away but her voice paused him. "I'm sorry, Brooks."

He turned. The look she gave him was sincere. "I know. I appreciate the apology, though."

"I didn't mean to wreck your computer," she whispered, her tone sleepy. Compliant. A rare moment.

"You didn't, honey. We fixed it, remember?"

She nodded then cringed. "It was awfully loud."

"It was." Moving back, he perched on the edge of the couch and looked down at her. "You knew you weren't supposed to touch it, right?"

Her eyes darted right then left before shifting down. "Yes."

"Then why did you do it?" he asked, one brow arched.

"'Cuz I'm just like my daddy."

Brooks' internal radar spiked. "You're what?"

Skeeter's chin quivered, then firmed. "Grandma says I'm just like my daddy," she repeated, her tone sharpening. "And my daddy wasn't a nice man. 'She's Tom through and through, Rita, right down to the core,'" the girl mimicked, her voice tart. "'You'll have trouble with that one, mark my words.'"

Brooks' ire rose in her defense. "Skeeter, that's not true. At least, it doesn't have to be true." His mind spun, wondering what to say, what to do.

"My daddy did bad things. So do I," the girl declared, absolute.

Brooks smoothed the child's tousled hair away from her forehead. "Your father made some bad choices. Those weren't your fault, Aleta. Grown-ups make mistakes, just like kids."

"Do you do bad things?"

Leave it to a kid. Brooks scrubbed a hand across the base of his neck and wrinkled his brow. How do you explain the difference between criminal wrongdoings versus a lapse in judgment? He shook his head. "I've hurt people's feelings before. And I fought in a war."

Her eyes widened. "You did?"

He nodded.

"You were a soldier."

"Yes."

"Did you ever ride in a tank or a helicopter?" Her voice pitched upward.

"Lots of times. I thought you were sleepy."

"Not now." She stifled another yawn, her jaw stretching. "Do you have a uniform?"

He did but wasn't about to parade it out. "Packed away."

"Oh." She lay silent, thinking, her fingers grasping the teddy tighter. He wondered what was coming. He didn't have long to wait. "Did you ever have a little girl, Brooks?"

A flash of Amy, pregnant with Paul's child, flashed through his brain, but the regret wasn't sharp like it used to be. "No."

"Oh."

She sounded disappointed. He tilted his head. "Why?"

She shrugged and looked away. "'Cuz maybe your little girl would want to be strong and good like you."

He clasped her free hand and squeezed. "Maybe she would. But I would love her no matter what. I would help her learn to be good, but I'd love her no matter what she did."

"Really?"

"Really, truly."

"Are you like your dad, Brooks?" Again she yawned. This time her lids settled closed, then quivered open.

"Yes and no. My dad loved working with wood. I do, too. But my dad was never a soldier and I did that for a long time because I loved it. We're all a mix of our moms and dads, honey. But we make our own choices of what we do, good or bad."

She narrowed her eyes then let the lids relax. "Then maybe I'll be good, Brooks."

Her simplicity inspired his smile. "That would be nice, Aleta." He watched as she eased into sleep, his mind going a mile a minute.

She thought she was bad because she was like her father. Of all the foolish notions. Once more he grasped the back of his neck, squeezing lightly. He'd run her declaration by Rita, tell her what the girl said. Maybe they'd finally gotten a glimpse of why she behaved the way she did.

Watching her sleep, the dark lashes a smudge against ivory cheeks, a surge of protectiveness pressured his chest. Seven years old, a little bit of a thing, certain she was destined to be evil because she was a chip off the old block.

One way or another, he'd show her that was untrue. Build her faith in herself, in the goodness God gave her.

As he stepped away, he eyed the child and the computer once more. No, he wouldn't head back to the shop today, not after the near disaster that morning. For the moment, watching Skeeter was a full-time job. One he didn't mind nearly as much as he thought he would.

Chapter Twenty

"Rita, this is so pretty." Sarah Macklin spun in a little circle, arms wide, her smile bright as she surveyed the front room of the bakery the next week. "I love it."

Rita's grin widened. "I have to pinch myself every time I walk in. Isn't it marvelous?"

"Wonderful." Sarah moved along the wall, her fingers trailing the wainscoting with its chair-rail molding. Sunny yellow paint brightened the upper walls, a mélange of photos and paintings offering a homey touch. White eyelet curtains framed the broad front window, magnifying the effect. "I love these shots of historic buildings."

"Amazing what you can do with a digital camera and a good computer, isn't it?"

"It's lovely. The whole effect invites people in. You guys have done a great job. I'm only sorry I haven't had time to help. And that I keep stealing Brett to work on the farm."

Rita brushed that off. "We've had plenty of help from friends in AA and Craig. I can't believe they got all this done so quickly."

"Seriously? With Brooks leading the brigade?"

"Good point. You can stay for coffee? Try out the new service? I just installed the cappuccino machine. Which means I unboxed it and plugged it in."

Sarah laughed. "I can't. Too much work right now. Next

month, once the baby's here. Or some night. Duty calls in the form of sheep and puppies."

"Understood." Rita gave her a hug, stepped back and smiled at Sarah's growing midsection. "Not long now."

"I know." Sarah smiled as she passed a hand across her previously flat belly. "I love it. But this baby tends to slow my steps around the farm. I don't have quite the leverage I used to. I thank God for Brett and the Bristol boys every day. Their help is the only thing keeping me going right now."

"And they're more than happy to do it," Rita assured her. "All right, you go. I'm going to finish up here and head for home. It's been a long day."

"Yes it has, but I'm grateful for the longer hours of daylight. It makes my life easier."

"Me, too."

Rita finished setting up packing supplies, stocking bright white shelves with flat cardboard boxes of all shapes and sizes. Brooks had ordered tables and chairs from a downstate supplier at cost, slated to arrive tomorrow. The baking supply cabinets were being stocked daily as orders came in. Sacks of sugars, basic mixes and tubs of colored icings lined the far wall while boxes of frozen specialty items stocked the freezer. The big mixer held a place of honor at the opposite end of the work area, strategically positioned near a drain for hosing down.

She'd hired Abby Byler to help out on the counter, a cute Amish girl who'd come by a few days ago. It might be tight, opening with just three people on board, but until she had a better idea of volume, she couldn't go hog wild. And Sarah and Liv would be there to help opening week, along with a couple of the gals from AA. Manning the front counter for speedy service was vital in those openings days. Baking could be done all night. Customer service? You only got one chance to make that good first impression. Rita was bound and determined to do just that.

Tired but more than a little grateful for this long-awaited opportunity, she shut off the lights, stepped outside and locked the door.

"Rita Slocum?"

Rita turned, surprised, a niggle of alarm snaking her spine. She'd come out the back door like she usually did, behind Higby's Hardware, the Dumpster-lined alley a good place for her car, leaving more customer parking on Main Street.

A woman faced her, ragged and worn.

"Yes?"

"I'm Melanie Hillman."

Rita scoured her memory banks and came up short. "I'm sorry, I don't—"

"Remember me."

Rita shook her head. "Have we met?"

"On paper."

Now Rita felt totally lost and more than a little nervous, the woman's gaze penetrating, her tattered appearance out of step for the area. The few businesses that backed up to the alley were closed for the day, the late-spring sunset shadowing the narrow drive. "I don't understand. Do you need something?"

"Not anymore. Already lost it. But thanks for asking."

Fear coursed more freely now, the woman's attitude almost menacing. She jerked her head toward the bakery behind Rita. "This your new place?"

"Yes."

"Isn't that special?" Melanie took a step forward, her gaze raking Rita's clothes, her hair, the new business. "Very special. And it must feel good to have the cash to fund something like this, to have your husband bilk innocent people out of their life savings and still have the nerve to set up a brand-new business right in front of our faces, rub our noses in your success."

The light dawned. "You were one of Tom's clients."

"Fools is more like it, but it's nice to see that although some of us lost our homes, our families, our job and our dignity, you came out smelling like a rose, all prim and proper with your high-end blue jeans and pretty little bakery. Bet that feels good, doesn't it?"

Her home? Her family? Her job? Had this woman really lost it all?

Guilt seized Rita's midsection and clutched tight.

Melanie wasn't just a statistic on paper, a faceless name on a lawyer's list. Before Rita stood a living, breathing human being whose life had been turned upside down by Tom's greed.

"How can I help you?" Rita fought back fear and moved down a step.

"Help me?" Melanie offered a bitter laugh, then indicated her appearance with a wave of her hand. "I'm beyond help."

"No one is beyond help."

"I am."

Her words heightened Rita's fear and guilt. "Where do you live?"

"Right here."

"Here?"

Melanie stared at her, daring Rita to misunderstand, then slid her gaze to the Dumpsters across the alley. Rita swallowed hard. "You're homeless."

"Thanks to you."

"But I—" Rita was about to explain she had nothing to do with Tom's business, with his clothes, with his deceit, but staring at Melanie, words escaped her. Melanie's plight was as much her problem as anyone's. "There must be something I can do. Some way to help."

"Think about me." Melanie shifted back and forth, restive, eyes darting. "When you open your sweet little store every morning, think of me back here. And when you bake pretty cakes with pink and yellow roses, think of me back here. And when you take racks of fresh bread out of your big expensive ovens, think of me back here."

"You can't stay here."

"You kicking me out? That's rich."

"No, I didn't mean it like that," Rita explained, fluttering her hands, nerves making her stumble through the explanation. "But you can't live huddled under an overhang behind the Dumpsters."

"Can and do." Melanie stepped back, thrust her chin forward and jerked her head left. "That's my place, my Dumpster. You gonna take that away from me, too? Well, why not? You've already taken everything else, haven't you?"

I've taken nothing, Rita wanted to cry out. *Not a blessed thing. I've struggled, cried, tanked and then rose from the ashes, and it took years.*

As Melanie slipped into the shadows, Rita saw her right hand shift from beneath her oversize coat. She raised a brown bag to her mouth and drank, the gulping action making Rita's mouth water.

Now Rita recognized what seemed so familiar about Melanie. Her appearance mimicked what Rita had seen in the mirror for two long years. The waxen skin, hollow eyes, gaunt cheeks, dull hair. Recognizing that, Rita's entire being longed to stretch out a hand and grab that bottle, let the wash of sharp, hot whiskey dull the pain Melanie brought to the surface.

Who was she fooling? Staring at Melanie's shuffling retreat, Rita saw herself, her real self, needy and dependent.

She slipped her hand into her pocket but her fingers met nothing but cotton lining and a bit of lint. No chip. She must have forgotten it off the dresser that morning in her hurry to get to work before coming over here to stock shelves.

And what was the chip but a stupid old metal disc, anyway? A cheap medallion that said out of thirty-eight years on the planet, she'd actually done something right for one. How pathetic was that?

Fear and longing gripped her heart as shadows deepened, night chasing day with cooling temperatures.

Melanie's plight plagued her. How insensitive was she? How buried in herself? Tom's victims were real people whose lives had been hideously altered by his actions. Why hadn't she sought them out, tried to make amends?

Because she was so busy drowning her sorrows in booze that she let her life fall apart, neglecting her children, her home, herself, her friends. She took the easy way out, but wasn't that what she did best? Appearances, all the way, just like her mother.

Melanie had disappeared, but the sight of her, bottle tipped, sweet reprieve from reality flowing into her, set Rita's salivary glands working overtime.

One drink. Just one. Just enough to take the edge off and soften the angst, cushion the blow of reality Melanie represented. Just one nip of eighty-proof anything, enough to smooth the rough edges Melanie's encounter raised.

Call Kim. Now.

Rita climbed into her car and withdrew her phone, fingers fumbling for the speed dial. Kim's number went straight to voice mail, meaning her phone was off for some reason. Most likely she was at the hospital with her mom.

Brooks.

Should she call him?

Embarrassment flooded her, shame cutting deep.

What would he think of her, when a simple thing like watching someone slug rotgut put her in such a state? Why couldn't she be strong like him? Like Kim? Why was her commitment so shallow while theirs loomed mountainous?

God, I need help here. Serious help. I watched that woman's face, the pain, the suffering, the bad choices she's made and I saw myself, weak and unkempt, anger and sorrow making choices for me.

I've hurt people, Lord. I might be putting on a good show now but I've hurt people badly. My kids, my family. And Tom's victims have been little more than names on a paper to me for the most part.

Melanie's accusations came back to her.

Rita put the car in gear and drove around front. The bakery windows shone like jewels in the reflected streetlights, the white curtains pristine in their newness.

She didn't deserve this. Any of this. She'd crashed and burned with no thought of others, wallowing in grief, shame and guilt. Now she stood on the precipice of a dream come true, her own bakery, a respectable businesswoman in a beautiful town.

Guilt seized once more, and from Rita's vantage point on Main Street, the opportunities to pop into one of the college bars were noticeable. And who'd know?

Do not fear for I am with you, do not be dismayed, for I am your God. I will strengthen you and help you; I will uphold you with my righteous right hand. Rita's heart leaped as she thought of the words.

God knew. First, last and always, ever present, ever watchful, God had been her strength, her support, her go-to through all this. Hadn't He given her multiple opportunities to strengthen herself? To mend the wrongs of her past?

But—

There were no buts. Images of Liv, Brett and Skeeter filled her mind, their growing independence in tandem with hers.

Once again her fingers probed her empty pocket, longing for the comfort of her chip, its tangible mark of progress.

Change the things you can.

A police cruiser pulled alongside and a nice-looking young man lowered his window. "Need help, ma'am?"

Did she ever.

She sent him a wan smile and motioned to her new enterprise. "I'm opening this bakery in a few days and I think I'm a bit overwhelmed."

His grin eased her. "Well, we've got lots of folks just waiting for you to open those doors, my wife among them. Her name was Cissy Annucci and you made every cake she ever had, from the time she was just a baby. Just today she said she can't wait to pass that tradition on to our kids."

His words sparked hope. "Really? I remember Cissy and her brothers. And her mom, Mary Anne."

"My mother-in-law wouldn't hear of anything for a party unless it came from Rita Slocum."

Affirmation that she hadn't screwed up her entire life maybe? Just the past few years?

"You have a good night, ma'am. Nice meeting you."

"You too, Officer."

She regrasped the phone and punched the speed dial for Brooks. He answered on the first ring. "Hey, what's up? It's late for you to be calling."

"I'm having a little trouble, big guy."

He switched modes instantly. "Where are you?"

"Outside the bakery but headed your way."

"You okay to drive?" Unspoken question: Have you been drinking?

"I'm okay. But I need you."

"I'm here."

"Ten minutes."

He was outside waiting when she pulled up, pacing, the woodcrafting store closed and quiet, the parking lot empty. Pal trotted alongside as if sensing trouble. She'd barely put the car in Park before he pulled the door open, reached in and hauled her out, holding her, hugging her, the beat of his heart a steady reminder of strength and support. "What happened?"

"It's a long story."

"Then come inside. We'll talk. You okay?" Brooks stepped back, worry washing his features, brow furrowed, his face pensive. She met his gaze. Concern deepened his gray eyes to slate, his expression a mix of anxiety and love.

Staring up at him, she saw his affection plain as day and knew she mirrored the emotion. He looped an arm around her shoulders, hugged her into his side and led her into his living room. Pal circled a few times, his tiny whine wondering what was wrong. He settled in once they sat, his chin resting on extended front paws, his dark brown eyes anxious.

Brooks pulled up a chair across from her, handed her a cup of her favorite tea and leaned in. "What happened?"

She told him, the feel of the mug and scent of the tea relaxing her. He listened well, an established sponsor, occasionally interrupting with an observation or question. By the time they were done Rita felt better. Much better. Brooks grasped her hands. "Why did you hesitate to call me when you couldn't get Kim?"

Rita faltered a moment, averting her eyes. He waited, chin dipped, until she was ready. "I felt like scum."

He nodded, not interrupting.

"Seeing Melanie was like holding up a mirror."

"An old mirror."

She acknowledged that with a grimace. "Not so old and not pretty. I was embarrassed not only by what Tom had done and how clueless I've been about the aftereffects, but just seeing her made me see myself and I felt…" She pulled in a deep breath and sighed, then dragged her gaze back to his. "Cheap. Unworthy."

"We've all felt like that, Reet. I can relate."

"You can't, Brooks. Not really." She faced him squarely, wanting to be honest, knowing it was harder because of her feelings for him. For him, above all others, she wanted to appear special. Be special. In reality, she was just another drunk, living day to day. "Everyone here knows what a strong man you are, how you conquered your demons and turned your life into an example for others."

How he wished that were true. "Rita, I—"

She stood and shouldered her bag. "I let down my family. My parents. My kids. I let myself sink into oblivion and wasted two years of their lives. Now I've got a mother who second-guesses everything I do and kids who worry every day that I'll do something stupid."

This was exactly why he could never sponsor her. Try as he might, he couldn't separate his protective feelings from his actions. A part of him longed to comfort and shelter her; another part knew she needed to test her wings. With testing came pain. As much as he wanted to, he couldn't protect her from everything.

"Who has woe? Who has sorrow? Who has strife? Who has complaints? Who has needless bruises? Who has bloodshot eyes?" The biblical proverb explained the perils of overindulgence thousands of year ago. Drunkenness was an old problem with few new tricks to solve it. Faith. Hope. Abstinence. Fairly simple unless you were the drunk in question.

She moved to the door.

He followed, Pal padding alongside. Rita smiled down at the dog, stroked his head and sighed before bringing her gaze back to Brooks, the smile not quite reaching her eyes. "Thank you for being here."

He wanted to hug her but her words held him back. She thought he made a fine leader by setting a good example but Brooks knew he lived a lie. Until he reconciled the past, he had little hope for the future. "Call if you need me. If Kim's still tied up at the hospital, that is. Or if you just need a friend."

"I will."

He watched her go, a shadow in the soft light, small, still unsure, her growing self-esteem not strong enough to handle everything life threw her way. But it would be, Brooks assured himself. She'd made huge strides in a short space of time. She didn't have the option to run like he had, not with three kids and no funds, so she'd toughed it out.

Now if only he could say the same about himself.

Chapter Twenty-One

Brooks glanced up as Tootsie entered the wood shop the next morning, his second cup of coffee not enough to soften the edge of a sleepless night. Concern for Rita had him second-guessing his scheduled trip to Baltimore, or maybe was he looking for a reason to delay the trip. Either way, sleep deprivation had him more than a tad on edge. "You're early."

She nodded, her expression unsure. "Can I see you, Boss?"

Amused and puzzled, Brooks glanced around. "You're not seeing me now?"

A tiny smile quirked her mouth, but it disappeared instantly. "I need to talk to you."

Brooks stood. "Of course, Toots. What is it?"

She scrubbed her hands down the sides of her pants and faced him square. "I'm pregnant."

Brooks stopped dead. "Excuse me?"

She nodded, biting her lower lip. "Pregnant. The baby's due in December."

Brooks' mind spun.

This girl had worked for him for well over three years. Nearly four. He thought he knew her. Now here she was, telling him she was expecting a baby in a few months' time. Unmarried, but engaged to a soldier serving in Iraq. But Matt hadn't been home in almost a year. Brooks frowned. "When was Matt—"

"He wasn't," she interrupted, not allowing him to finish.

Realization steamrolled him. If Matt hadn't been home, that meant...

Brooks stared, the tumblers slipping into place. Seeing her nervousness, her hands twisting in front of her thickened waistline, he was transported to a different young woman explaining how she carried another man's child.

His brother's child.

He couldn't speak. All he could see was Amy, twining her fingers, explaining it couldn't be helped. She loved Paul and would marry him that week.

Brooks turned to stone inside, much like he'd done long years before. In Tootsie's face, her expression of guilt and remorse, he faced Amy all over again.

He couldn't separate the two women, not with Paul and Amy on his mind these past weeks. Paul's prognosis, his guilt at not fixing things sooner. It bubbled up, welling over, threatening to explode from him much like it had in that Baltimore bar twelve years before.

"Boss, I—"

"Get out."

"I—" Once again she tried to speak but Brooks couldn't hear it. Wouldn't hear it.

Didn't anyone stay true to their vows anymore? Mean what they said? The overhead light danced across her kneading fingers, the glint of the left-hand ring mocking the pledge she'd given a fine young man. "I'll mail your last paycheck. Go."

He disregarded the hurt on her face. She turned, tears slipping down her cheeks. At the door she swung back, her mouth open as if to say something.

The look he gave her squelched it. Wide-eyed, she stared at him, then turned and let herself out the door.

Emitting an angry bellow, Brooks seized the shelf he'd been smoothing. With a javelin thrower's arc, he hurled it across the workspace, the maple board gouging a hole in the plastered wall before tumbling to the floor.

More. He wanted to throw more. Needed to throw more.

Break things, disrupt the ordered pattern of the fine machinery in his workrooms. The studied organization scorched him, laughing at the control he'd worked so hard to maintain. Hadn't he prided himself on his better judgment, his tolerance?

There was no tolerance now, just a bitter taste as he pondered the plight of PFC Matt Dennehy, a soldier who'd pledged his life and honor to a woman that cheated on him.

Bile threatened. Mick appeared for his shift, his ever-present backpack slung across one shoulder. With slow and deliberate moves, he stepped into the workroom, an eyebrow arched. "What's going on?"

Brooks couldn't answer. Shaking his head, he pushed by his apprentice and stormed out, leaving before he destroyed everything he'd built.

He strode to his truck, brushing by Liv without acknowledging her. He needed to get away, breathe fresh air. Maybe walk the river, settle himself down. He didn't think of his Bible or the problems of those ancient peoples. He only saw the here and now as he climbed into the cab.

His cell phone jangled. He picked it up but refused to answer the out-of-town number. He knew the caller. Knew him well. And at this moment, he didn't need Greg Callahan spewing niceties of how he should forgive and forget. Come home. Signal the all's well. He silenced the phone, staring at its glowing face.

A moment later a text appeared. Just two short words. Two short words that sent the pickup truck aiming for the liquor store rather than the river's path.

Paul's dying.

Rita spotted Tootsie's tearstained face and grabbed her in a hug. "Honey, what's wrong?"

"He fired me," Tootsie blubbered, her sobs choking the words. "He looked at me as though I were evil incarnate, then told me to get out."

"No."

Toots nodded tearfully. "Yes."

Rita's mind spun. She knew Brooks. At least she thought she did. She understood his faith, his upright stance. He was a man of firm direction and strong beliefs. But coupled with that was a rare understanding of man's frailties. Hadn't she witnessed that time and again at AA meetings? Brooks handled everything with compassion and common sense, a combination that helped others achieve what he had. A normal life, a day-to-day existence without dependence on alcohol.

Why would a man whose empathy embraced a roomful of strangers on a regular basis turn on a young woman who'd been his friend and employee for years? Because she was pregnant? It made no sense. Were certain mistakes less forgivable than others? Didn't Christ challenge the crowd that gathered to stone the adulteress? Didn't he leap to her aid in quiet fashion, equating her sin with theirs, leveling the playing field?

Rita shook her head in bewilderment. "Are you sure you understood him, honey? That doesn't sound like—"

She didn't have a chance to finish the statement. Tootsie puffed a strand of hair away from her face and offered, "It's hard to misconstrue 'Get out. Now.'"

Rita groaned inside. Toots was right. Not much leeway there. "I'm just finishing up here. Let me grab my purse, we'll figure this out."

"I don't know how."

Neither did Rita but she had to try. Less than twenty-four hours ago, Brooks had been her rock. And now? She had no clue.

"Can you go to my place and keep an eye on Skeeter when she gets home? And take Brett to his soccer game tonight?"

Toots nodded. "Yes."

Rita grabbed her in one more hug before climbing into her car. "Chin up. We'll fix this."

Tootsie's doubtful expression said she wasn't so sure but Rita had to believe there was a way. As Tootsie turned north, Rita called the wood shop, hoping. Praying. Liv answered.

"Hi, honey." Rita worked to keep her voice calm. "Can I talk to Brooks?"

"He's not here." Liv sounded worried. "He ran out this morning and took off in the truck."

"Making deliveries?" Rita asked, but she already knew the answer.

"No. He told Mick he had to get out of here and took off. He didn't look right, Mom. He didn't even speak to me. And Tootsie's not here, either."

"Tootsie's going to our house to watch Skeeter and take Brett to his game tonight. I'm going to find Brooks."

"Okay."

Rita hated the hint of uncertainty in Liv's voice. How she wished her kids had never had to deal with the craziness of addiction and self-absorption.

But that's over now, she assured herself. Isn't that what Brooks had reminded her of last night? An old mirror, he'd said, and he was right.

She'd worked hard to wipe that image clean, change her ways, one day at a time. Now if only she could offer Brooks the help he'd given her.

Chapter Twenty-Two

❧

"Go away."

The snarling voice inside the apartment didn't dissuade Rita. She knocked again, glad he'd come back home from wherever he'd disappeared to earlier. "Open the door, Brooks."

No answer. She tried the handle. Locked. The store was locked as well, with Mick and Liv gone home, so there was no access to Brooks' home through the inner entry. Rita drew a breath, muttered a prayer and knocked again. "Please, Brooks."

A long silence followed her entreaty before heavy shoes sounded across the floor. The lock disengaged. Brooks swung the door just wide enough to frame himself in the opening. "What?"

She looked up at him. He was disheveled and rumpled, blatantly out of character. She longed to reach out, smooth his hair. Adjust his shirt collar. The expression on his face kept her hands at her side. "I want to help."

"You can't."

"Have you been drinking?" The sharp smell of blended whiskey tainted the air.

"I would if you'd leave me alone."

"I'm coming in."

"No, you're not." A firm hand blocked her path, Brooks'

expression a mix of anger and concern. "There's booze in here."

"So?"

He cursed as he scrubbed a hand over his jaw. "Woman, I haven't spent the past year keeping you sober just to hang it all up tonight over some two-bit tramp who never meant a word she said."

"Now I'm confused and worried," Rita asserted, taking advantage of the tirade to slip by him. "Tell me what this is all about, Brooks. And don't go near that whiskey or I'll—"

"You just broke the basic rule of sponsorship," he chastised, flexing his hands. "You're supposed to let the drunk make the choice of sobriety on their terms and then you support that choice. You don't order them around."

"Welcome to sobriety school, Rita-style," she retorted. "What in the world has gotten into you? Tootsie comes to you to confess her mistake, already carrying a truckload of guilt along with an unborn child, and you go off on her, fire her, then take off for places unknown scaring everyone, holding a grudge against a girl who's done nothing but work hard for nearly four years. What's up with that?"

"You don't know what you're talking about, Reet. Go home." He passed a tired hand across his face then shouldered by her. "This fight's got nothing to do with you. Or Tootsie, for that matter."

"On the contrary," she spouted, following him. "It's got everything to do with me. We care for each other. We have everything going for us, Brooks," she entreated, moving close to his side. She reached out a hand to his sleeve. "Don't shut me out. Don't drink. Don't make us start all over again. Please?"

She fought the threatening tears and worked to keep herself objective.

Nearly impossible. She realized why only certain people succeeded as AA sponsors and why she'd never be one of them. Kim had always been able to steer her to all the reasons she didn't want to drink and that method worked.

Rita? All she could do was beg. *Lame,* she scolded herself.

But at the moment nothing else came to mind. Gripping his sleeve, she dropped her eyes and uttered a prayer. "God, I know You're with us. I know You hold Brooks in the palm of Your hand. I know You see his strength and his righteousness. But You also see his pain, dear Lord, and it's a pain he refuses to share. Help us, Father. Help us work this out. Ease his anxiety. Please."

Brooks stood still during her prayer. The moment it was done he ushered her to the door. "You need to go. I can't trust myself right now."

She thrust her chin up and planted her feet. "I trust you."

"You have no idea what you're saying."

"I do. I'm an intelligent woman, Brooks. You've told me that often enough. I trust you to keep me safe. Out of harm's way."

"Leave. Please."

"No."

Once more she nudged by him, moving into the living room. Pal padded up to her, his doggy face woeful as if wondering what all the fuss was about.

A sudden inspiration hit her. She'd switch things up. Turn the tables. Knowing Brooks like she did, Rita was sure he'd sacrifice himself to save her. She took a bracing breath, squared her shoulders and turned. "Where's the bottle, Brooks? I think I need a drink."

"No." In a move rivaling laws of physics, he blocked her path, saving her from herself. "That's not an option, Rita."

"Oh, I see." She stared him down. He squirmed but stood his ground. "It's an option for you but not for me? Well, forget that. If I want a drink, I'll have a drink."

"I said no." He grasped her upper arms with powerful hands. The look on his face was nothing to trifle with.

"And I said yes." She met the look head-on, daring him. "You won't listen to reason, won't talk things out and won't let me share your burdens, so why not just get wasted together? A couple of old friends, tying one on."

He pulled her into his chest, holding tight. "This isn't the way to do it, Reet," he muttered, his voice thick. "You're supposed to talk me down, step-by-step. Make me see the difference between the choices. Offer me an alternative."

She started to cry. "I am," she murmured, tears dampening the front of his wrinkled shirt. "I'm your alternative. Don't slip off the wagon, Brooks. Don't do anything that would mess us up. I love you."

"Shh." A heavy hand stroked the back of her head, giving her a hint of hope. "It's all right."

She pushed back. "It's not. I know that. But I can't help if I have no idea what I'm fighting. Or who. What drove you to this? What pushed you over the edge? Tootsie?" At his change of expression, Rita shook her head. "But why? I know what she did was wrong, but why is it more wrong than every other sin we commit? I'm a sinner, Brooks. Will you turn away from me?" The thought that he might chilled her. Love without forgiveness simply wasn't love.

He stepped away, his expression pained, his hands fisting. "Sit down. Please." He softened the command with the last word. When Rita perched on the edge of the sofa, he drew a chair closer and settled into it. For a moment he clasped and unclasped his hands. His eyes darted to the open bottle, his expression dark. Then, with a deep breath, he faced the moment of truth he'd dreaded.

"I told you I was engaged once."

She nodded.

"Her name was Amy. Is Amy," he corrected himself. "We were young and in love, or thought we were. We got engaged, I got redeployed and Amy sat home waiting." He stared at his hands, rubbed Pal's head, then sighed. "I didn't know then what it took to be a good man, what I needed to do to be a good husband. I reenlisted, believing what I was doing for our country was important, that it made a difference. In short, I was gone too long."

"She found someone else."

He nodded and huffed out another breath, then grimaced. "My brother."

"No."

"Yes. My older brother Paul is a minister, a sweet, gentle man, my polar opposite."

Rita stretched a hand to his knee. "You're a gentle, sweet man, Brooks Harriman, and don't you forget it."

A ghost of a smile softened his features. "I've improved. Anyway, Amy met me at the airport and not only broke our engagement, but explained she was carrying Paul's child and they'd be married the following week."

"And you freaked."

"To put it mildly. I started drinking, guzzling actually, and couldn't get my head around how I'd put my life on the line day after day and Paul got the girl. It pulled our whole family apart because I couldn't see how my parents could possibly forgive Paul and Amy when I was the injured party. I tumbled so far down into the well that I lost myself in booze."

"What brought you around?"

His face shadowed deeper. His eyes darkened. The hand stroking Pal's head paused. "The night their little boy was born I got sucker punched in a bar. Bad timing on that poor drunk's part because I was spoiling for a fight. I wailed on the guy, Reet. Nearly killed him."

"Oh, Brooks."

"The police came. A tough Cherry Hill cop named Greg Callahan hauled me to jail, dried me out and gave me an option to be booked or join AA."

"I like him already."

"I figured why not? This guy would never know if I came to the meetings. Baltimore's a big city, I could just nod and agree, gain my release and lie low for a while in another neighborhood." Brooks shrugged. "But on the way home an old woman stopped me. She handed me a prayer book. Never said a word. Just took my arm, looked me in the eye and handed me the book."

"What was in it?"

He turned to meet her gaze. "The Serenity Prayer. So I went.

Figured if God wanted me there *that* badly, it would be rude not to show."

Rita smiled.

"Greg was there. And he became my sponsor. He's a big part of the reason I live here now. He told me it would be smart to move to a place where I wasn't besieged by memories at every turn."

"I'm glad. If you'd stayed there, we'd never have met."

"True enough. Paul and Amy got married, his congregation forgave him openly, citing the powerful attraction of young love, they had a baby boy and then a couple more kids and lived happily ever after. Until now."

"Now?" Rita frowned. "Why? What happened?"

"Paul's dying."

"No."

"And I need to go there. See them. Make amends."

"You never went back?"

"I meant to, but…" He sighed and scowled, knowing he was a loser. "No."

"Oh, Brooks. All this time lost."

"Tell me about it." He stood and paced away, ran his hand through his hair, then swung to face her. "When you came in here last night you said you were embarrassed because Melanie reminded you of what you'd been, what you'd done."

"Yes."

"I've had twelve years of sobriety, Rita, but I still struggle with the choices I've made. Letting the years slip by, hurting my family time and again. Every Christmas, every Easter, every birthday. I've lived a lie all these years, pretending to be something I'm not. Strong." He snorted in disgust at himself, ashamed. How could he possibly commit to this fine woman and her kids if he could turn his back on his family for over a decade? Pain knifed through him.

"You need to go."

He knew that, just like he understood that the woman before him, a woman with three great kids, needed someone totally vested in them, their lives, their best interests. Although the locals lauded him as a man of strength and character, he knew what he was. A slacker. "I know."

"So do it."

"As soon as the bakery is ready."

She stood and moved beside him, her gaze firm, her voice taut. "I couldn't live with myself if you stayed here to finish up while your brother lies sick in Baltimore. The bakery doesn't need you nearly as much as he does. And what if something happens and you blow this chance at reconciliation?"

"And if they hate me? Despite all these years of sobriety and hard work? Can I handle that rejection, Reet, even though it's well deserved?"

She pressed her cheek against his arm. "No one could hate you, Brooks."

Brooks wasn't so sure. More than once he'd hated himself. "I wish I were as certain."

"Leave your gift there in front of the altar. First go and be reconciled to your brother, then come and offer your gift." Rita quoted the verse from Matthew softly, the words falling on him like gentle rain.

Could it be that easy to wash himself clean by simply facing the past head-on? Or was his shameful behavior unforgivable? There was only one way to find out and precious little time left to do it. "I'll head out on the next flight."

Rita rose and hugged him. "I wish I could go with you. Be with you."

He wished the same thing but knew she needed to be here to open the new store as promised. New business owners couldn't afford to disappoint the public. He hugged her back. "Me, too. Can you watch Pal for me?"

"Glad to."

She gathered up the dog's things then jerked her chin toward the kitchen. "Dump the bottle before I go."

"I won't drink."

"Nevertheless."

He nodded, admiring her temerity. She'd come a long way in a relatively short stretch of time. He hoped she understood how absolutely amazing that was. "All right." He moved to the kitchen and upended the bottle until every last drop was down the drain.

"Okay?"

"Yes." She turned her gaze toward his bedroom. "Need help packing?"

He shrugged. "I travel light."

Rita cast a glance around the bare-essentials apartment. "Like that's a surprise. Book your flight, leave me a list of what needs to be done and we'll get it done. All the major parts are in place. Now it comes down to me and the machines."

He walked her to her car. Pal jumped into the front seat, always ready for an adventure, his look imploring Brooks to come home soon. He settled the dog then walked around to Rita's side of the car. "You'll be okay without me?"

She read the meaning behind the words, a mix of concern and hope. "We'll get by. I'll be praying for you. Every step of the way."

He nodded and stepped away, his normal confidence shaken. But then so was hers. She cared for this man, loved him in fact, but the thought of turning her back on loved ones for over a decade had her questioning her judgment. A woman with three kids couldn't afford to take chances on their health, happiness and well-being, especially when she'd already jerked them around.

Pulling away, she watched him fade in her rearview mirror, green leaves dancing in the soft May breeze. His figure grew slight as the distance increased. Glancing back, she felt as if he was fading from her life in the very same fashion.

Brooks tossed his single bag into the truck and headed north down Route 11. Knowing the plane out of Syracuse to Baltimore was in the early afternoon, he recognized his time constraints. But if he was planning on fixing the mistakes in his life, he'd start right here, right now. He pulled up to a small apartment complex, hopped out of the truck and rang Tootsie's bell. She answered the door, surprise and shame vying for her features.

He grabbed her in a hug and held tight. "I was a jerk and I'm sorry. Forgive me?"

She laughed and cried, a habit he hoped would end with the birth of the kid. "You don't hate me?"

"Never. You're like family to me." He didn't miss the irony that he'd managed to treat his family even worse.

Oh, yeah, he had things to fix. Things to change. And hopefully the courage to do just that.

"You forgive me?" He leaned down to see her face, hoping she knew just how bad he felt.

"Of course." She stepped back, dabbed her eyes and gave him a playful swat. "Aren't you supposed to be catching a plane?" Obviously Rita had called her already.

"Couldn't do it until I made things right with you. And if you need anything—" Brooks swept her midline an encompassing look "—anytime, you let me know. No hesitation. Got it?"

"Got it."

He smiled and tousled her curls. "I'll call you guys, let you know when I'll be back."

"We've got your back, Boss. I take it this means I'm hired again?"

He flushed. "With a raise. So if you don't have anything to do, I've got a store that sure could use your expertise while I'm gone. And after."

"I'm on my way."

He took a deep breath, nodded and headed back to the truck.

Chapter Twenty-Three

Change the things you can....

Rita fingered the chip in her pocket and looked around the bakery, her checklist in hand, missing Brooks like crazy but figuring it was high time she stood on her own two feet.

Within reason, of course.

"This is absolutely wonderful, Rita."

She turned, amazed, the sound of her mother's voice a total surprise. "Mom? What are you doing here?"

Her mother handed her a huge floral arrangement that matched the bakery's decor. "We're here to help with the grand opening."

Quick tears sprung to Rita's eyes. Her mother saw them and grabbed her in a hug. "I'm sorry, Rita. Truly sorry. I've said and done some things these past few years that I can't undo, but I'll try to do better. I promise."

"But how?" Rita turned as her father walked in wearing an apron.

An apron.

"Reverend Slaughter reminded me of something I'd forgotten, a psalm he quoted. 'He gives the barren woman a home, making her the joyous mother of children.' It made me realize I hadn't acted joyous in a very long time."

"So we talked," her father joined in. "And we've decided to be joyous."

Rita couldn't help it. She giggled.

Her mother beamed. "See? It's working already. Now I figure you've probably got things well organized, but I know how to box and tie baked goods, so if I just stay out here and help the gals on the counter, I can be useful and part of the fun."

"Oh, my goodness." Rita grabbed them both in a hug. "I can't believe you're here, but you've just made this the happiest day of my life."

Her father's grin showed total agreement. "I figured I'd be a greeter and gopher. You've got quite a line forming out there, and it's only getting longer by the minute. Skeeter has agreed to be my partner in exchange for playground time later."

Skeeter returned his smile and grabbed his hand. "There are lots of people out there, Mommy. Grandpa and I are going to talk to them while they wait."

"I see that." Trepidation snaked up her spine. She forced it down. "We've got tons of backup, the ovens are full, Liv and Kim are putting the finishing touches on things and Sarah, Abby and I are working the counter." Brooks' example had shown her it was good for the owner to be on hand, filling orders, shaking hands during busy times. She could lose sleep baking when the sun went down. Right now...

She smoothed clammy hands across her apron. "Let's open the doors."

Their walkie-talkies hummed throughout the day. "We need muffins."

"Got 'em loaded. Sending the cart now."

"Danish soon. Any kind."

"We're on it."

"Cookies, please. We've had a run on chocolate chip and snickerdoodles with sprinkles."

Kim laughed through the handheld device. "I told you people would love those. Total kid cookie."

Rita grinned as she boxed a buttercream-frosted chocolate cake for Mary Anne Annucci, the kind police officer's mother-in-law. "You were right."

As she handed the middle-aged woman the box, Mrs. Annucci grasped her hand and leaned forward. "I'm so proud of you, honey."

Tears sprang to Rita's eyes, the words a surprise and her emotions already teetering on the brink. "Why?"

"Because you're brave. And strong. You've got what it takes to do good."

"Mrs. Annucci, I—" Rita struggled for a response that wouldn't sound totally insipid. She hadn't been brave at all. She'd been weak. Self-indulgent. Then she crashed and burned.

The older woman squeezed her hand and winked. "It's easy to give up, to fall by the wayside. The hard thing is to stand back up and fight, to take control. You're a fighter, Rita."

"Thank you."

Rita's mother stepped closer and hugged Rita's shoulders, bobbing her head in agreement. "That's my girl."

"And mine!" her father called from the door, grinning as he shook each customer's hand, his small talk easing the extended waiting time, typical of an opening day.

And what an opening day it was.

Brooks called midday. "I won't keep you, I'm hoping you're swamped with people, but I had to know. How's it going?"

"Beyond my wildest hopes and dreams."

"Excellent."

"My parents are here."

He laughed. "Really?"

"And having a wonderful time. I feel like I'm living in an alternative universe and any minute now I'm going to wake up."

"You're awake and doing exactly what you should be doing. You've changed the things you can."

In a nutshell. "With help."

"That's what friends are for. Gotta go. I'll call you later, catch you up."

"Okay."

She hated to hang up the phone, that little connection with Brooks meaning so much, but there was work at hand. *God, bless Brooks with the patience and the wisdom that he uses with us every day. Help him find even ground with his family, come to terms with his old life. And then bring him back home to me. Please.*

Brooks hesitated at the front door. It felt strange to reach for the doorbell on a house he'd called home for thirty years, but wrong to let himself in. Greg Callahan solved the dilemma for him. With an aggrieved sigh, he reached forward, pushed open the door and called for Brooks' parents. "Carol Ann? Bill? I've brought something for you."

"Greg, how nice."

His mother's voice pulled Brooks back in time. As she rounded the corner to the living room, a white dish towel flapping in her hand, she stopped dead, her face draining at the sight of her younger son.

Uncertain, Brooks stood stock-still. His instinct was to grab her into the hug he longed to give, but he wasn't sure he had that right anymore. He'd tossed a whole lot away over a decade ago and she'd been part of the baggage.

Regret swept him anew. Deepened lines on her face reflected the passage of years. Her hair, gray at the edges, still glowed a soft honey color, just like his. She wore green khakis and a pullover shirt that read Grandma Knows Best surrounded by spring blossoms. She looked absolutely beautiful.

"Brooks." In a flash she was on him, her arms around him, no hint of hesitation in her response. "You're home. You're here." Hugging him and laughing, she pulled him into the room without ceremony, calling as she did, "Bill! Come see what Greg brought us."

"Some of that crusty bread from the Italian bakery, I hope." As Brooks' dad came down the stairs at a quick clip, father and son locked eyes.

Bill's gaze went from welcoming to cautious. The two men regarded one another as the older Harriman descended, his footfall more measured. Once at the bottom he paused and angled his head. "Son."

Brooks stepped his way, trying to assess his father's feelings. His dad wasn't as tall as he used to be. That hurt. He gave him a respectful nod. "Yes, sir."

Bill Harriman shifted his look to Greg. "You did this?"

"I told him about Paul. He came back on his own."

"I see." Bill looked Brooks over, making an assessment. With a start, Brooks realized that's where he'd inherited the art of sizing up people and situations at a glance. He'd never made that connection before.

And the stubbornness. He saw it in the old man's eye, the tilt of his chin. Seeing his father's stance, it was all Brooks could do to stand motionless, not head for the hills. He was safe in the North Country. No backlash. No reminders.

Reality smacked him upside the head. Lately everything had been a reminder. Being with Rita and her kids reminded him of how much he'd missed with his enforced isolation. But loving Rita brought to mind the pain he'd suffered with Amy's betrayal and his subsequent alcoholism. For a man who'd made his living taking chances, he'd turned into a turtle. Life in a shell was safe but carried a lousy vantage point, something he wanted to change. Could he, when just sensing his father's mixed feelings set his heart hammering?

"Your brother's very ill." Bill drew a deep breath and creased his brow, his expression protective. "I don't know how much he can take, Brooks."

He was talking old wrongs. Brooks knew it. He nodded and stretched out a hand to his father's arm. "I didn't come to fight, Dad. I came to make peace. And see you." He encompassed his mother with his look, then brought his gaze back to his father. "I've missed you guys."

"And Amy?" His mother stepped forward, her expression warm. "Will seeing her be all right? You've forgiven her?"

"I forgave them a long time ago, Mom. About the time I grew up enough to shoulder my share of the blame. I'm just too stubborn for my own good."

"You get that from your father," she answered, chin bobbing, her voice tart. "And since you're here and it's usually Paul's good time of the day, I say we hop in the car and head over there, pay him a visit."

Now?

Brooks breathed deep and nodded, ignoring the adrenaline rush, his drumming heart. "I think that's a great idea."

"Now I know I'm dying." Paul's voice was surprisingly strong for a man who looked so weak. If Brooks hadn't been told this was Paul propped against the pillows of the hospital bed, he'd never have known it. Thin wisps of faded hair framed tired eyes. Sallow cheeks deepened the look. A volunteer from the church rolled her eyes and smiled at Brooks.

"Pastor hasn't lost his sense of humor, has he?"

Brooks shook his head as he approached the bed. "I guess not. How're you doing, Paul?" Instinctively he ignored the chair and dropped to his knees alongside the pillow. With a gentle hand he smoothed the sparse shock of hair from Paul's forehead. "You've looked better, old man."

Paul grinned and lifted a frail hand to cover Brooks' stronger one. "Outside, perhaps. Inside, I'm much stronger than at our last meeting."

Brooks didn't want to think of their last meeting, the awful things he'd said. He swallowed hard and looked into the gray-blue eyes of his older brother. The same brother who'd taught him to hold a bat. Shift his weight. Tuck his chin, eye on the ball.

Tears gathered in Brooks' eyes. He blinked them away but not before Paul noticed. "You always were a crybaby," he teased, his voice rasping.

"You picked on me," Brooks returned, a smile chasing the tears.

"Only until you were bigger than I was," retorted Paul, his hand grasping Brooks'. "That was about fifth grade."

"That meant I had ten years of catching up."

A smile curved Paul's lips. "And you tried."

"Oh, yeah." Once again Brooks passed a hand over his

brother's forehead. "Can I get you anything? You thirsty? In pain?"

"No." Paul shook his head, his eyes locked on Brooks. "No, just having you here. That's enough. I need your forgiveness, brother."

"No, you don't." The lump reformed in Brooks' throat, choking him. His Adam's apple convulsed. It took effort to squeeze the words around the obstruction. "I need yours."

Paul's head sank back. He blinked, then turned his eyes back to Brooks. "I was weak back then."

The irony wasn't lost on Brooks. His brother's frail body lay feeble now but Paul had gained strength where it counted. His spirituality shone through dimmed eyes. Brooks angled his chin in admission. "I wasn't nearly as strong as I thought, either."

"You were," Paul argued. "Our sin brought you down and I hated myself for that. For a while I hated Amy, too. I blamed her." At Brooks' look, Paul shook his head, his breath pulling. "It was easy to make her the temptress. I even found scripture that backed me up."

Once more Paul struggled for air. Brooks leaned forward, concerned. "Shh. It's all right now. It was a long time ago."

"Sin doesn't disappear with time. If anything, it grows into a soul-eating monster."

His words went straight to Brooks' heart. Hadn't he found that out firsthand?

"I sought God's forgiveness a long time ago. And Amy's," Paul added, his expression softening at the mention of his wife's name. "But I need yours, Brooks."

Brooks grasped his brother's hand in a gentle grip. "When Jacob died, he sent his sons back to Joseph, to ask forgiveness for the wrongs they did him. Joseph not only forgave them, he assured them God used a bad situation for good."

"And has he?" Paul searched Brooks' look. "Has he brought you good, Brooks? Given you a full life to replace what I stole?"

"You didn't steal Amy," Brooks corrected. "I know that now. If I'd treasured her like I should have, there wouldn't have been room for another man. And, yes, God has given me grace. Love. Fulfillment."

"You're married?"

Brooks shook his head. "No. But I hope to be. I'd like you to meet her."

"Better bring her fast," Paul shot back, teasing, but then concern darkened his features once more. He grasped Brooks' hand tighter. "Say you forgive me. Please."

"I do." Brooks brushed his hand over his brother's forehead. "But I need to hear it back. I said terrible things. I hurt our parents because they didn't choose me over you. They wanted us both and I couldn't deal with that. There was a lot of pride and selfishness inside me, Paul. I'm ashamed of it."

"No." Paul shook his head. "Be ashamed of your behavior, but your inner strength made you a great soldier. A fine wood-crafter. No, Brooks, I wouldn't trade that strength of yours for anything. You blessed our family with that power, that fortitude."

"You know I'm a cabinetmaker now?" Brooks wrinkled his brow. "How?" With a start, he huffed out a breath. "Big-mouth Callahan."

"He kept us up-to-date. Have you seen Amy yet? Or the kids?"

Brooks shook his head. "Will my being here upset her?"

"Absolutely not."

Both men looked toward the door. Amy stepped in, an older Amy, still lovely but looking frazzled by the day's events. "Your being here makes everything okay, Brooks."

He rose to shake her hand, then hugged her instead. She batted at him, tears flowing, then stepped back, saw the muddle she'd made of his shirt and didn't resist when he hugged her again. "I'm sorry, Amy. So sorry."

He wasn't sure what he was apologizing for but she seemed to understand. "I know. Me, too. It's been a long time, Brooks." She stepped back, grabbed some tissues and dabbed her eyes and nose. "How's our patient doing?"

She moved around the other side of the bed, sliding the chair forward to be near Paul's face. "Hey, darlin'. You got company while I was gone, huh?"

"He just showed up, out of the blue," Paul teased, sliding a mischievous look Brooks' way. "I *had* to be nice to him."

"Well, of course, at this stage of the game," Amy agreed, her smile mixed with unavoidable sadness. "Not a time for holding grudges, is it?"

Paul laughed and laid a hand against her cheek. He turned to Brooks. "She's kept me honest, no matter how self-righteous I wanted to be. It wasn't always easy."

"I expect not." Brooks motioned to the door. "I'll head out now, give you guys some time."

Amy looked up at him. "Thanks for coming, Brooks." In her eyes he read the time frame and it slowed his heart.

He nodded, then turned to Paul. "Anything you need a brother for? Anything I can get you?"

"Tickets to tomorrow's home game."

"Really?"

Paul nodded. "I'd like to catch one more and the weather is supposed to be mild enough. I don't handle cold all that well right now."

He didn't have to say anything further. They'd grown up watching the O's, cheering them on, earning money any way possible to afford the ticket price.

Brooks' heart went heavy with inevitability. One more game. That's what it came down to. How much time had he wasted on stubbornness and pride? He met his brother's gaze and gave a firm nod. "Consider it done."

Chapter Twenty-Four

Rita sank into the chair opposite her mother and breathed a happy sigh. "An amazing day."

"You can say that again." Judith wriggled her toes, tucked her feet beneath the adjacent cushion and smiled. "I haven't had that much fun since…ever."

Rita laughed. "But you've got to be tired."

"It's a good tired, you know?"

Rita knew. "Have I thanked you enough for coming?"

Her mother waved that off. "Our pleasure. It's so nice to see you doing something you love so much. And do so well."

Her mother's compliment made the day that much sweeter. If only Brooks could have been here, been part of what he'd worked so hard to create.

"What's wrong?"

Rita knew it was as good a time as any to fill her mother in. "My friend Brooks, who you heard so much about today?"

"The one that sounds like a combination superhero and statesman? The man who can do no wrong, according to your children, and the owner of the greatest dog in the world?"

Pal perked an ear and thumped his tail as if recognizing his part in the conversation.

Rita smiled. "The very one. He's gone to Baltimore to face some things in his past, and his brother's dying of cancer. I hate that he's doing this on his own, facing it alone. As his friend, I should be there. Heaven knows he's been my support time and again, so I feel bad that I'm up here and he's down there."

Her mother's understanding expression smacked of maternal appraisal. "You love him."

Rita sighed, sipped her tea and sent her mother a chagrined look. "That obvious, huh?"

"You lit up like a Christmas tree every time his name was mentioned today, which was fairly often. So, what are you waiting for?"

"Huh?"

Her mother tapped her watch. "Dad and I are here to take care of the kids, you have all day tomorrow and the airport's only two hours away. Get in your car and go. You don't reopen until Tuesday, so that gives you all day tomorrow in Baltimore, you fly back Monday to bake for Tuesday. Simple."

It *sounded* simple, but after confronting Brooks last night Rita couldn't help but wonder if seizing the upper hand with a surprise approach was the best of ideas. The dynamics of Brooks' family sounded fairly convoluted. What if her presence only added fuel to the fire?

"If you second-guess yourself too much, you'll chicken out." Her mother whisked a debit card from her purse. "My treat."

"Mom, I—"

"Time's wasting." Her mother leaned forward, her face earnest. "Consider it part of my joy-spreading pledge."

Reading the sincerity in her mother's gaze, Rita gripped the card and stood. "I'll grab my bag."

Her mother's words added speed to her steps. "Now that's my girl."

"Brooks, can you hand me that light blanket, please?"

"Got it."

Brooks handed over the team fleece, the black-and-orange oriole holding center stage. Amy tucked it around Paul's lap, ignoring his protests. Brooks squatted to his level as the rest of the family found their seats. "I don't remember her being this bossy."

Paul slipped his gaze from Amy to Brooks and back. "Comes with age. Ow! You're not supposed to hit a dying man."

The blanket edges tucked to her satisfaction, Amy shifted back and graced them both with a dour look. "It was barely a tap and you know it. And you—" she turned more fully Brooks' way "—weren't here often enough for me to boss you around. I've spent all these years making up for it by nagging him."

"Yeah, thanks," Paul muttered. He winked at Brooks then turned, scanning the seats, the box, the stadium. He drew a deep breath and let it out slowly, an easy smile brightening his features, relieving the stress of illness fleetingly. For just a moment, the baseball cap covering his lack of hair, he looked like the Paul of old, sitting in the park, a mitt in hand to snag foul balls, the ball park's all-American peace almost tangible.

Baseball. Hot dogs. Apple pie.

Rita.

Brooks hadn't been able to get her off his mind since she walked out his door the other night. What was she thinking? Doing? Could she possibly know how much he cared?

No. He hadn't told her. He'd hung back, knowing he had to make peace with his family. But had he hesitated too long? And would she see his pigheadedness as too big a hill to hurdle? Rita had more than herself to consider, she had three beautiful kids whose well-being rested on hers.

Seeing his father and mother, watching Amy with Paul, Brooks knew what he wanted despite his best efforts to sidle away initially.

He wanted a family, *Rita's* family, and maybe, just maybe…

He wasn't even sure he dared hope for more than that, not with the time he'd wasted.

Regret washed over him. He should be with her now, celebrating her opening, the apex of years spent dreaming and planning.

But no amount of military training taught him how to be in two places at once. He bit back a sigh as the team took the field for batting practice. He stood and rooted with the rest of the early fans, then turned to sit back down. "Hey, Troy, isn't this your seat, buddy?" Brooks waved a hand to the empty seat adjoining his.

Paul's oldest son scanned his ticket and shook his head. "No, this is mine."

"Nope."

"Yours?" Brooks shifted his attention to Caleb, their second son.

Callahan must have messed up the seat count. Understandable with a big family, but it felt funny to have the seats around him filled and the one alongside obviously vacant.

Ah, well. No big deal. His mother touched his shoulder from behind. He smiled, patted her hand, then leaned down to grasp the bucket of popcorn he'd set on the concrete riser.

"Actually, I believe that's my seat, big guy."

He upended the popcorn in his haste to get upright. Popped kernels landed here, there and everywhere, the flurry of buttered snack drawing looks from all around them. "Rita?"

He jumped to his feet, grabbed her in a hug and held tight, half-afraid he was dreaming and would wake at any moment.

But no. She felt real and smelled better than real. The soft silk of her hair slipped across his cheek, through his fingers, the essence of fruity shampoo and buttered popcorn delighting his senses. "You're here."

"Well, I had a day free, so…" She twinkled a gaze up to him, met his and nodded, one hand touching his cheek, his hair. "I'm here."

"But how?"

She frowned, pretending misunderstanding. "A plane?"

He blew out an exaggerated breath. "No, I mean how did you know we'd be here? At the ballpark?" She raised her gaze and Brooks didn't even have to turn. "Callahan."

"I tracked him down at the station by telling him I had an AA emergency. He called me right back and for a stick-in-the-mud old cop, it's delightfully simple to get him to spill the beans."

Greg leaned down. "I figured if it wiped that mopey look off your face, we'd all be better off, so I bought an extra ticket and invited her to the game. Which appears to have been a pretty good idea on my part."

Brooks hugged her again and laughed up at Greg. "The best idea, by far. Hey everybody, I want you to meet—"

"Hey, Rita, nice to meet you."

"Rita! So glad you could come."

"Rita." Carol Anne Harriman grasped her hands, squeezed her fingers and smiled. "That was my grandmother's name, dear."

"Really?"

"Mmm-hmm. How lovely to have it in the family again."

"In the family?" Rita turned, surprise and anticipation spiking her heart rate. What had Brooks shared with them?

"Are you going to be my aunt?" A little girl Skeeter's age tugged the hem of Rita's fleece. "Because Brody Phillips has an aunt and I'd like to have one, too."

"I...um..."

Brooks dropped to one knee and grasped her hand, his move spiking delight through the entire box of baseball fans. "Rita, I know this is a touch unreal and slightly unexpected, but that's marked our path from the beginning, right?"

Blinking back tears, she clenched his hand and nodded.

He grinned. "Would you do me the honor of becoming my wife, letting me father those beautiful children? And any others God might send our way?"

Heart racing, Rita leaned down a smidge but kept her voice loud enough for others to hear. "How exactly are you planning to raise a baby while you run a wood shop?"

His grin deepened. He squeezed her fingers once more. "I figured you'd raise the kid while running a bakery. When it comes to kids, cookies and cakes beat finger-eating power tools, right? At least for the first decade or so."

She burst out laughing, imagining growing old with Brooks, his steady warmth and humor a cornerstone in her life. But... in for a penny, in for a pound. "And we'd be married at Holy Trinity, right? The same church where we'll attend services together each and every Sunday."

He laughed this time. "If you say yes so I can get up, I'll even sign up to usher. This concrete's a killer on old knees."

"Yes."

His grin softened to a smile as he rose. "Really?"

"Absolutely, big guy. It's the only way I can think of to get custody of the dog."

He burst out laughing again then kissed her, his embrace assuring.

"They're getting mushy."

"I think it's sweet."

"Yuck."

"Hush, you two. It's nice."

Amy's approval was seconded by Paul's. "Um, excuse me for interrupting the moment, but if you guys want me to officiate this thing, might I suggest a really short engagement?"

Rita stooped down, Paul's humor drawing her in, his gleam of inner faith belying the outward weakness. She reached out a hand to shake his, meeting his gaze with a wink and a smile. "Hi. I'm Rita. I'm going to marry your brother. And yes, I know he's stubborn, bullheaded, cocksure and fairly arrogant. For reasons only God can explain, I find that combination irresistible."

Paul grinned.

"So, if you could find time in your busy schedule to fly up to Grasse Bend, we would be honored to have you officiate."

Paul slanted his gaze to Brooks. "You have finally met your match, and high time, too."

Brooks grinned. "I can't disagree. And she comes with a made-to-order family, so once again, it's a win-win."

Rita's smile met his, her pledge of life and love evident for all to see. "It certainly is."

Epilogue

Judith Barnes clutched an already scrunched hanky to her face as she walked into the bridal room of Holy Trinity, afternoon sunlight streaming through the stained-glass windows, the bent light dancing rainbows on the far wall. "Oh, honey. You look beautiful."

"Do I?" Rita met her mother's gaze in the mirror while she tried to ward off an attack of nerves with little success.

Liv stepped in from the adjacent changing room, smiled at her grandmother and sent Rita a scolding look. "You know you do, Mom. That dress is gorgeous. Brooks will be totally over-the-top when he sees you."

"He already is."

Brooks.

He moved into the room looking calm and self-assured, while Rita's heart jackhammered her pulse into overdrive. He grasped her hands and angled his head, a hint of humor brightening his eyes. "Nervous?"

She drew a breath. "Yes."

A slight frown wrinkled his brow, his gaze penetrating, his focus fully on her. "Second thoughts?"

"None."

A warm smile eased the look of concern. "That's good. I'd hate to have to eat all that cake myself."

His quick relief said he'd been worried about her and he'd

broken the rules of convention to make sure she was okay. Her heart melted at the loving warmth in his look, the gentle grasp of his hands on hers. "Listen, soldier, I made the cake, I get the cake. You could have the napkins or something."

He laughed and leaned down, his soft-spoken words for her ears only. "I love you, Reet. I'd like to spend the rest of my life showing you that. Night and day."

His words soothed. The tickle of his breath against her cheek, her ear, brought thoughts of forever-after at his man's side, in his arms.

She smiled, relaxing. "I'd like that, too. And I was only kidding about the cake."

"Yeah?"

"Of course." She nodded, grinning now. "I'd have left you half to feed your family. I like them. A lot."

He laughed. "Well good, because the feeling's mutual. Great dress, by the way."

"Which you're not supposed to be seeing now," scolded Rita's mother, but her smile assured him it was all right.

"And you," Brooks looked over at Liv and nodded his appreciation, "look absolutely lovely. You're gorgeous, Liv."

She flushed, pleased. "Thank you, Brooks."

"Brooks!"

Skeeter barreled into the room with no thought of patent-leather shoes or her sage-green chiffon flower-girl dress. Brooks scooped her up, kissed her cheek, then noted Brett and Greg Callahan headed their way.

Skeeter cradled his cheeks. "Thank you for bringing Pal to the wedding."

"Pal?"

Brooks frowned, met Greg's gaze and lifted a brow.

Brett raised his hands, palms out. "He's sitting at the back door, calm as can be."

"But how?"

Rita touched his arm. "Did you forget to latch your doggy door?"

Brooks' expression was answer enough.

Rita turned toward Brett and Greg. "And he's behaving?"

"Pal always behaves," Skeeter announced, her look firm. "He's a very good dog, isn't he, Brooks?"

Her sincerity sparked Brooks' grin. "He certainly is. In fact, if Greg wasn't already my best man, I might have considered having Pal put his paw print on the license."

"Brooks." Skeeter laughed at him, grabbed his face between her two small hands, gave him a sweet kiss and laid her head against his shoulder in a gesture of total acceptance. "You're funny."

"Thank you, Skeeter." He kissed her back and flashed Rita a slightly bemused look of love and laughter. "We're good?"

She nodded.

Brooks cast an obvious look around the room, jutted his chin toward the entry where the dog waited patiently and asked, "You know what you're getting into, right?"

Rita laughed. "Better than most. Do you?"

His look said he couldn't be happier. "Absolutely." Still holding Skeeter, he leaned in for one more quick kiss. "I'll meet you down front, okay?"

"Very okay."

He set Skeeter down and headed out with Greg and Brett. After a few steps, he paused and turned, catching Rita's eye. "We did it, you know."

Rita angled her head, puzzled.

"Changed the things we could. With help." Brooks raised his gaze heavenward, then smiled and winked.

His words put it all in perspective. They'd traveled a broken road, riddled with wrong turns. Potholes. Mistakes.

But the road ahead looked much smoother because they'd travel it together, a family rooted in faith and fun. Rita nodded, met his grin and pointed to the wall clock. "Don't you have someplace you're supposed to be?"

He grinned and nodded before heading back down the hall. "See you in five."

Her mother burst out laughing. "He's a god guy, Rita."

Liv agreed as she straightened the hem of Rita's gown. "He is. He makes Mom laugh all the time."

"And me, too," cut in Skeeter, her face serious.

The three women exchanged knowing looks of agreement. On a scale of one-to-ten, Skeeter's improved disposition was off-the-charts good.

Her grandmother laid a soft hand along Skeeter's cheek, leaned down and nuzzled a kiss against her hair. "I hear your music, honey. You ready to start things off?"

Skeeter smiled, nodded and grasped her grandmother's hand. "I'm ready, Grandma."

The sight of Skeeter and her mother working together almost undid Rita's new calm, but she drew a breath and nodded toward the vestibule, the sweet strains of music calling them to worship, to vows, to the promise of tomorrow. "Then let's go."

* * * * *

Dear Reader,

Most authors write from experience. Rita and Brooks' story is no exception. As the child of two alcoholics, I longed for the day when my parents would find AA, see the light and become sober. It finally happened when I was in my thirties, married with six kids of my own. Employing clever scheduling, my children never knew Grandma and Grandpa had a drinking problem until they were old enough to need to know. Until then, fairyland and gentility provided a better choice.

As a displaced teen I met a new girl at school. Her name was Bonnie. Bonnie's parents were both recovering alcoholics, and the warmth, love and welcoming atmosphere in her home was what I'd dreamed of. Their success inspired a story worth telling. My experiences with AA members taught me that help is a decision and a prayer away.

Addictive behaviors are tough to kick, especially if the body carries an inherent tendency to addiction. Add life's strife and you've got a recipe for trouble. But I believe we forge our destiny with God's help. While not necessarily easy, choosing strength is rewarding and a better choice for our families, friends and loved ones, but especially our children.

Thanks so much for choosing to read MADE TO ORDER FAMILY, a story encompassing the broken road that often leads to faith and love. Please feel free to e-mail me at loganherne@gmail.com, visit me at ruthloganherne.com or snail mail me c/o Steeple Hill Books, 233 Broadway, Suite 1001, New York, N.Y. 10279. I look forward to hearing your stories, your ideas and your thoughts!

Ruthy

QUESTIONS FOR DISCUSSION

1. Rita and Brooks share an addiction they've struggled to overcome. This makes their budding relationship risky on many levels. Should people with addictive disabilities chance the odds and form long-lasting commitments like marriage?

2. Brooks abandoned his family to come north and begin anew, unable to juggle a relationship with his parents while they still loved Paul and Amy. Was Brooks being fair or was he just doing what seemed necessary at the time?

3. As Brooks' recovery became stronger with time, he still didn't contact his family, make amends. He sees his long-standing aloofness as an outcome from Paul and Amy's relationship, but in reality, didn't the sin become his as well, for refusing to bridge the gap? Was his shame over that choice well-founded?

4. Rita's children have gone through a great deal of strife because of their parents' bad choices. Rita trusted her heart and instincts with Tom, and then chose alcohol to take the edge off her problems when they seemed insurmountable. Do you think it's harder to trust your instincts, your inner self, when you've made bad choices?

5. Skeeter's behavior is a catalyst to Brooks' story because Brooks likes order. Skeeter disrupts order. Brooks likes respect. Skeeter is disrespectful. Many second marriages involve children. What are some good guidelines for a potential stepparent to use before considering marriage involving another person's children?

6 Liv wants to work with Brooks because his wood shop calls to her artistic instincts. Do you think there are other reasons that draw her to Brooks' store?

7. Tootsie is reluctant to tell Brooks about her pregnancy because she recognizes his strong conservative ethics. She fears his disappointment and disrespect. Does waiting make things easier or tougher when she confesses her secret?

8. Brett is an adolescent boy who has to deal with his parents' public indiscretions and his little sister's brattiness. How does he manage this in a positive way?

9. Rita doesn't believe she deserves success or happiness. Her self-image is fractured by guilt. How does striving to open her own business, take charge of her life and take a big chance help to assuage those feelings of self-degradation? Does keeping her one-year chip at hand seem realistic, a token of success in a little metal disk?

10. As Brooks' feelings for Rita escalate, thoughts of his family press in. How are these two things linked in his mind?

11. Taking chances is serous business for alcoholics. They have to maintain constant awareness of their emotions, knowing disappointment and rejection might nudge them away from sobriety. What would it be like to have to weigh every decision against its outcome for the rest of your life?

12. Brooks' high regard for Tootsie is challenged when her story closely reflects his history with Amy. For a short while, his love for her is overwhelmed by his angst over Paul's illness, his own inaction and Tootsie's deception. How does God use circumstances to help us better deal with our own insecurities?

13. Rita opens her bakery without Brooks' physical presence, but his faith in her spurs her to make forward strides. Rita's parents use this opportunity to reaffirm their belief in her,

as well. How did Rita's push for her own autonomy inspire others' heightened respect?

14. God wants us to make amends with our brothers, our sisters. Brooks seeks to make peace with his family after a very rough night. How hard is it to go back home after all those years, admit your mistakes and make amends?

TITLES AVAILABLE NEXT MONTH

Available September 28, 2010

HIS HOLIDAY BRIDE
The Granger Family Ranch
Jillian Hart

YUKON COWBOY
Alaskan Bride Rush
Debra Clopton

MISTLETOE PRAYERS
Marta Perry and Betsy St. Amant

THE MARINE'S BABY
Deb Kastner

SEEKING HIS LOVE
Carrie Turansky

FRESH-START FAMILY
Lisa Mondello

LICNM0910

LARGER-PRINT BOOKS!

**GET 2 FREE
LARGER-PRINT NOVELS
PLUS 2 FREE
MYSTERY GIFTS**

Larger-print novels are now available...

YES! Please send me 2 FREE LARGER-PRINT Love Inspired® novels and my 2 FREE mystery gifts (gifts are worth about $10). After receiving them, if I don't wish to receive any more books, I can return the shipping statement marked "cancel". If I don't cancel, I will receive 6 brand-new novels every month and be billed just $4.74 per book in the U.S. or $5.24 per book in Canada. That's a saving of over 20% off the cover price. It's quite a bargain! Shipping and handling is just 50¢ per book.* I understand that accepting the 2 free books and gifts places me under no obligation to buy anything. I can always return a shipment and cancel at any time. Even if I never buy another book, the two free books and gifts are mine to keep forever.

122/322 IDN E7QP

Name	(PLEASE PRINT)	

Address		Apt. #

City	State/Prov.	Zip/Postal Code

Signature (if under 18, a parent or guardian must sign)

Mail to **Steeple Hill Reader Service:**
IN U.S.A.: P.O. Box 1867, Buffalo, NY 14240-1867
IN CANADA: P.O. Box 609, Fort Erie, Ontario L2A 5X3

Not valid to current subscribers to Love Inspired Larger-Print books.

**Are you a current subscriber to Love Inspired books
and want to receive the larger-print edition?
Call 1-800-873-8635 or visit www.morefreebooks.com.**

* Terms and prices subject to change without notice. Prices do not include applicable taxes. Sales tax applicable in N.Y. Canadian residents will be charged applicable provincial taxes and GST. Offer not valid in Quebec. This offer is limited to one order per household. All orders subject to approval. Credit or debit balances in a customer's account(s) may be offset by any other outstanding balance owed by or to the customer. Please allow 4 to 6 weeks for delivery. Offer available while quantities last.

Your Privacy: Steeple Hill Books is committed to protecting your privacy. Our Privacy Policy is available online at www.SteepleHill.com or upon request from the Reader Service. From time to time we make our lists of customers available to reputable third parties who may have a product or service of interest to you. If you would prefer we not share your name and address, please check here. ☐

Help us get it right—We strive for accurate, respectful and relevant communications. To clarify or modify your communication preferences, visit us at www.ReaderService.com/consumerschoice.

LILP10R

HARLEQUIN®

A *Romance*

FOR EVERY MOOD™

Spotlight on

Inspirational

Wholesome romances
that touch the heart and soul.

See the next page
to enjoy a sneak peek from
the Love Inspired® inspirational series.

*See below for a sneak peek at
our inspirational line, Love Inspired®.
Introducing HIS HOLIDAY BRIDE
by bestselling author Jillian Hart*

Autumn Granger gave her horse rein to slide toward the town's new sheriff.

"Hey, there." The man in a brand-new Stetson, black T-shirt, jeans and riding boots held up a hand in greeting. He stepped away from his four-wheel drive with "Sheriff" in black on the doors and waded through the grasses. "I'm new around here."

"I'm Autumn Granger."

"Nice to meet you, Miss Granger. I'm Ford Sherman, from Chicago." He knuckled back his hat, revealing the most handsome face she'd ever seen. Big blue eyes contrasted with his sun-tanned complexion.

"I'm guessing you haven't seen much open land. Out here, you've got to keep an eye on cows or they're going to tear your vehicle apart."

"What?" He whipped around. Sure enough, mammoth black-and-white creatures had started to gnaw on his four-wheel drive. They clustered like a mob, mouths and tongues and teeth bent on destruction. One cow tried to pry the wiper off the windshield, another chewed on the side mirror. Several leaned through the open window, licking the seats.

"Move along, little dogie." He didn't know the first thing about cattle.

The entire herd swiveled their heads to study him curiously. Not a single hoof shifted. The animals soon returned to chewing, licking, digging through his possessions.

Autumn laughed, a warm and wonderful sound. "Thanks,

I needed that." She then pulled a bag from behind her saddle and waved it at the cows. "Look what I have, guys. Cookies."

Cows swung in her direction, and dozens of liquid brown eyes brightened with cookie hopes. As she circled the car, the cattle bounded after her. The earth shook with the force of their powerful hooves.

"Next time, you're on your own, city boy." She tipped her hat. The cowgirl stayed on his mind, the sweetest thing he had ever seen.

Will Ford be able to stick it out in the country
to find out more about Autumn?
Find out in HIS HOLIDAY BRIDE
by bestselling author Jillian Hart,
available in October 2010
only from Love Inspired®.